Owl Light

by

Vonnie Winslow Crist

Pole to Pole Publishing
Baltimore

OWL LIGHT

Published by Pole to Pole Publishing
2nd Edition
Cover layout copyright © 2018 Pole to Pole Publishing
www.poletopolepublishing.com
Cover art "Owl Watches Intently Illuminated By Full Moon On Halloween Night"
copyright © rcreitmeyer

ISBN-10: 1-941559-24-7

ISBN-13: 978-1-941559-24-6

"Not Seen" ©2002 Vonnie Winslow Crist. *September Eleven Maryland Voices.*
"A Salem Town Great-Granddaughter" ©2017 Vonnie Winslow Crist. *The Great Tome of Magicians, Necromancers, and Mystics.*
"Harvest Mouse" ©2010 Vonnie Winslow Crist. *The Welter 2010.*
"Gifts in the Dark" ©2009 Vonnie Winslow Crist. *Dia de los Muertos – A Day of the Dead Anthology.*
"The Burryman" ©2011 Vonnie Winslow Crist. *Ocean Stories.*
"By the Sea" ©2009 Vonnie Winslow Crist. *Tales of the Talisman.*
"For the Good of the Settlement" ©2007 Vonnie Winslow Crist. *Space Westerns.*
"At the Asian Arts Center" ©2009 Vonnie Winslow Crist. *The Chesapeake Reader.*
"Henkie's Fiddle" ©2010 Vonnie Winslow Crist. *Potter's Field 4.*
"On a Midwinter's Eve" ©2011 Vonnie Winslow Crist. *Tales of the Talisman.*
"Kingdom Across the River" ©2011 Vonnie Winslow Crist. *In the Garden of the Crow.*

Library of Congress Control Number: 2018935156.

Praise for Owl Light

"*Owl Light* is a wonderful collection of short stories and poems that transports the reader from the past and into the future, peering into the mysterious, twilight hours of the human experience. Highly recommended!"

– David Lee Summers, author of *Owl Dance* and
The Astronomer's Crypt

"*Owl Light*, a collection of stories and poems united by the theme of eventime and owls, is a rich tapestry of magic and ritual. What delights the reader in this anthology is the way Crist can apply fresh eyes to a familiar situation and conversely, can present the unfamiliar as if it were an old friend. The reader has a series of surprises in store as the collection charts the calendar of life through seasonal rituals. My all-time favorite moment was the shock of recognition—and amazement—when the Three Billy Goats Gruff made a cameo appearance in a totally unrelated situation. As I said—the familiar through fresh eyes."

– Jonathan Shipley, author of stories published
in *Sword and Sorceress, After Death, Stories from
the Near-Future, Tales of the Once and Future King,*
and other books.

"Vonnie Winslow Crist's intriguing collection *Owl Light* is a fascinating juxtaposition of poetry and prose—fairy tales new and re-imagined, modern myth and ancient ritual. Her stories span galaxies and eons. And tying them all together are the owls, those mysterious denizens of twilight and legend. There is something to resonate with all readers within its pages."

– Rie Sheridan Rose, author of
The Conn-Mann Chronicles

"A quiet darkness pervades Crist's stories and poems. There are owls, too, of course, watching over fantastical worlds of ancient tradition and time travel. If you let the tales lull you to sleep, expect shining eyes to peer from the forest of your dreams."

– Anne E. Johnson, author of *Things from
Other Worlds* and *Exit Code.*

Books by Vonnie Winslow Crist

The Chronicles of Lifthrasir
The Enchanted Dagger
Beyond the Sheercliffs

Novelette
Murder on Marawa Prime

Story Collections
Owl Light
The Greener Forest

Children's
Leprechaun Cake & Other Tales

Poetry Collections
River of Stars
Essential Fables

Table of Contents

For Ernie,
Tim & Dawn, Phil & Kristin,
Nathaniel & Gabriel, Melissa & Aria,
and
all those who believe in
the mystery & magic of owl light.

"In Owl Light, that darksome time
when creatures of the shadows move among us,
how easy it is to believe in the mysterious and magical."

Vonnie Winslow Crist

Owl Light

Owl Light

Be daring:
push wide the door
when sun vanishes in a puddle of pink,
temperatures chill,
and twilight creatures emerge
from cracks, crevices, caves, and hidey holes.

Be audacious:
step onto the porch
when skies darken to indigo,
frogs serenade,
and beings of Faerie slip
from beneath tree roots, rocks, and bridges.

Be fearless:
descend to the yard
when moon raises her ghostly face,
dogs howl,
and phantoms venture
from swamp, sea, and cemetery.

Be courageous:
walk towards the forest
when early stars flicker,
owls wake from slumber,
and shadows appear
where shadows ought not be.

But be cautious, dear ones,
for dusk dims to darkness
as surely
as dreams change to nightmares,

and dawn
is more distant than you know.

The Clockwork Owl

*A*s *many of the timepieces in his shop clanged or chimed* noon, John the Third looked up from the back of a mantle clock he was repairing to see a strange man walk through the doorway. Strange was perhaps the wrong word, though there was a strangeness about him that made John the Third uncomfortable. The man was dressed much like many others who strolled up and down Water Street, occasionally darting in and out of businesses. His top hat, scarf, coat, gloves, vest, trousers—even his face, had a blend-into-the-background quality to them. But his gray eyes gleamed in a way John the Third had never seen eyes gleam.

"May I help you?" he asked the man.

The man pursed his lips, tilted his head slightly, and removed his gloves. "I have need of a watchmaker," he said.

"The men in my family have been makers of quality timepieces for seven generations. And I carry on the family trade, so perhaps I am the person you seek."

"Perhaps." The man stepped closer, removed a packet of folded papers from inside his coat, and then, handed them to John the Third. "Can you make this?" he inquired.

John the Third untied the string that held the bundle together, unfolded the papers, and carefully smoothed out the drawings.

Meticulously sketched and labeled in black ink with a draftsman's hand, were the directions for constructing a clockwork instrument of some sort. He noted the instrument's motor was powered by a mainspring wound up via a ratchet device with a key. Finely drawn were a complex series of springs and gears, small wheels linked by gear teeth, that redirected the motion in the wind-up mechanism diagrammed. Even the escapement was inked in clearly. And each part's measurements, down to the tiniest detail, were included.

"I believe this is within my ability to construct." John the Third rubbed his chin as he continued to study the drawings. "Watches are my specialty, and this..." He lifted the sheets of paper and searched for the appropriate word.

"Owl."

The man with the gleaming eyes had stepped closer. With his right hand, he pulled his gloves through his left hand again and again. He was obviously high-strung, but this small gesture was the only outward sign of his nervousness that John the Third noticed.

"Yes, owl." John tapped the diagrams with his forefinger. "I either have or can make all the parts save..."

"I have brought that part with me." The man reached inside his trousers' pocket and produced another bundle. This one was wrapped in what appeared to be some sort of cured skin.

Calf-skin, perhaps. Or lamb's skin. John swallowed hard. As he handled the skin he thought about the young animal that had been killed for its hide. Inside the skin was a tiny box. Five of its sides were brass, but the last side was made of a glass-like material. Using his spectacle loupe, he observed there were minute perforations at regular intervals in the glass. He adjusted his headband and leaned a little closer to the brass box. Behind the glass, there appeared to be a tiny machine of a sort he had never seen before.

"What does the box do?" John the Third asked as he sat up and moved the eye loupe lens up to his forehead.

"It is of no concern to you." The man replied. "The box shouldn't impede the function of the automaton." He cleared his throat. "Or the clockwork owl, if that is your preference."

"It is the same mechanical device, whatever it is called," replied John as he studied the diagrams, then added, "This is really a wind-up toy rather than a clock."

"It should not matter. Though you're a clock maker, you have already built one automaton," said the man as he plucked a small strand of thread from his herringbone vest.

John stood. "How do you know that?" His uneasy feelings about the stranger now seemed well founded. "I completed the dog yesternight. I have shown it to no one."

The man hesitated, gazed at the diagram, then raised his glinting eyes and stared at John. "Because I researched the historical files to find a clock maker capable of manufacturing an owl automaton. Yours was the only name I could find in the correct time and location who also made clockwork toys."

"So you are saying you're from..."

"I cannot state that. It is forbidden. But I can tell you that your wind-up dog is the first of many such clockwork machines you will make. I have come here—to this moment—to ask you to stop work on everything else and make my owl."

John the Third rubbed his forehead. Certainly the brass box on his work table was not like anything he had ever heard about. He was sure there were inventions on the Continent that he was unaware of, but in this city, jewelers, clock makers, and inventors alike would be buzzing about a miniature machine like the one before him.

"Tell me what it does, and why you need the owl so quickly. If you have all of time to..."

"But I do not," responded the man. His shoulders dropped. "Today, I have only a few more minutes. I will return in 10 days. Then, I will have a few hours. You see, I am here under false pretenses."

"I do not understand."

The man's demeanor became more sober. "Where I am from, I have worked decades to specialize in the technology of the mid to late 1800s. I am here to do research for a historical institute that uses time travel to understand past technology with the hopes it can be reworked to serve future needs. This morning, I attended a gathering of inventors and scientists to gather information for my employers, and must return to that event shortly. I leave for home as soon as the gathering concludes. But this owl," he pointed at the drawings, "is personal. It is why I studied the technology of your time for most of my life."

"Personal?"

The man nodded. "The machine in the brass box detects smoke and sounds an alarm. There will be a fire in your time that will burn to death two people. The grief from that loss will spill down the generations in the form of child abuse. More than one hundred and twenty-five years from now, a man will murder my older sister and nephews because of that fire. I am trying to prevent the deaths in this time and the murders in mine."

"Why not stop the fire from happening? Or put it out once it starts?"

"Rules. Regulations. Taboos." The man sighed. "To even bring that box, I had to bend rules. I can only travel with technology that's integrated into my body. To carry the brass box and its machine with me to this date, I had a piece of my skin removed and preserved. By wrapping the machine in my skin, I have attempted to stay within acceptable boundaries."

The clock maker grimaced, the idea of touching the tanned skin on his work table again repulsed him.

"I do not think anyone will return to undo what I hope to accomplish." The man pointed at the piece of his skin. "I have obeyed the letter of the law, even if I've circumvented its intent." He straightened his shoulders again, and put on his top hat. "But it can only be accomplished if you will help me. What say you, John the Third, will you construct the clockwork owl?"

"I am not sure if I believe your tale, but I think I can build the owl. As for the ten day time frame..."

"I will make it worth your while," said the man as he handed John a small sack that obviously held coins.

John opened the sack, dumped the money out on the tabletop, and gasped. The amount in front of him was twice what he earned in a year.

"When I return ten days hence, if the owl is ready for delivery, I will give you the rest of the purchase price."

Before John could protest the exorbitant amount, the man hushed him.

"For this sum, I buy the owl automaton and its delivery, in person, by you, to the address I give you, and your silence. In addition, if the owl is returned to you, I buy your assurance that you will remove the small brass box and destroy it. Afterward, the owl must be sent to the Boston address I will give to you when I return."

John silently calculated the time needed to construct the wind-up creature, then thought about what he could do with the money he earned from this job. He nodded, gathered the coins, and returned them to their sack.

"The clockwork owl will be ready and functioning when you return." He glanced down at the diagrams. "I just need a name to put on the order so..."

"Mr. Hopewell will do." The man said as he pulled on his gloves. "And should you fail to produce the owl automaton when I return..." Mr. Hopewell smiled a smile like a cat toying with a mouse. "Your life is forfeit."

"Wait, I didn't agree to..."

John the Third's protest fell on deaf ears as Mr. Hopewell walked out of the shop's front door.

§

*F*or what seemed like the hundredth time, John the Third stared at the entrance to his shop. He had worked day and night on the clockwork owl. He had used saws, files, polishing brushes, hammers and anvil, tweezers, gauges, the gold scale with troy weights he kept in a wooden box in the back room, and other tools of his trade to construct the brass wind-up toy ordered by Mr. Hopewell. The automaton perched on his work table was as close as humanly possible to the diagrams given him by the supposed time traveler. He was not entirely convinced the odd man with the glittering eyes came from the future, but the coins Mr. Hopewell had paid with were real—and that was all that mattered to the clock maker.

He had already spent the money. In addition to a few items he needed for the shop, John the Third had purchased the building. His father and grandfather owned their shop on the other side of the city, but he had only rented the two-story building where his clock and watch shop occupied the downstairs and John lived in the rooms upstairs. His lot in life had changed from struggling businessman to prosperous real estate owner in less than two weeks. And if Mr. Hopewell was true to his word, the final payment for the owl would allow John to make his intentions known to a certain seamstress who worked in a shop four buildings down on Water Street.

He wound the owl—just to check again that the brass bird was in perfect working order. The automaton responded by flapping its wings, opening and closing its beak, blinking its eyes, and shuffling forward in a most unowl-like manner. He chuckled. One could not help but laugh at the toy. And with the smoke-detecting machine securely fastened behind its left eye, John the Third hoped it really would save the life of two potential burn victims. Since fireplaces, coal stoves, oil lamps, and candles were used for heat and light in homes and businesses, fires were a common tragedy. He had witnessed the terrible burns suffered by people who had lived through their ordeal, and did not want to imagine the pain of those who had died.

He went to his shop's window and peered up and down Water Street. There was no sign of the man with the gleaming eyes who had ordered the owl. Still, it was early afternoon, so there was plenty of time for his mysterious customer to arrive. His patience was rewarded when his shop's chorus of clangs and chimes heralded the arrival of not only three o'clock, but also the clockwork owl's new owner.

"Welcome back, Mr. Hopewell," called John the Third from his work table as he motioned for his customer to come closer. He noticed the man had added a cane to his impeccable ensemble.

Mr Hopewell barely glanced at him. Instead, he studied the wind-up owl.

"Does it work?"

"See for yourself." John wound up the clockwork owl, set it on the tabletop, and let the brass automaton wobble about flapping its wings, opening and closing its beak, and blinking its eyes.

"Marvelous!"

John noted Mr. Hopewell could not refrain from smiling.

"I especially like the blinking eyes. Of course flesh and blood owls have three sets of eyelids—one for sleeping, one for keeping their eyes clean, and one for blinking like this little automaton here. Did you know that?"

"No," answered the clock maker. "And I am delighted I did not have to create three sets for this owl."

"I imagine you had enough work to accomplish without worrying about extra eyelids." Mr. Hopewell reached inside his coat and retrieved a sack and several pieces of paper. He handed the first slip of paper to John the Third. "This is the address where the owl is to be delivered by you at exactly five this evening."

The clock maker glanced at the address. It was in a well-to-do part of the city about a fifteen minute walk from his shop.

"And this is the card that goes with the owl," explained Mr. Hopewell as he gave John a calling card.

The clock maker read the hand-lettered note: *Please accept my apologies. I am unable to attend dinner, but I hope your daughter will enjoy this wind-up owl as a remembrance of her birthday. Cordially, M. Hopewell.*

"Lastly," said the man with the glinting eyes, "here is the address in Boston you must send the owl plus this slip of paper to, if the automaton is returned to you." He passed John the Third a scrap of paper on which was scrawled the name and address of a legal firm. Also on the paper were directions for the storage of the wind-up owl with journals already being held by the firm indefinitely for a Mr. M. Hopewell.

"And," stated Mr. Hopewell as he handed over a cloth sack heavy with coins, "here is the final payment. It should adequately compensate you not only for your work, but the cost of mailing the owl to Boston, should the need arise."

John the Third opened the small cloth bag, but did not empty its contents onto his work table. With just a glance he knew that the amount of money it contained exceeded the down payment made by Mr. Hopewell ten days ago.

He cleared his throat. "Thank you, sir. Your generosity has already changed my life. And this," John cradled the money bag in the palm of his hand, "will allow me to ask a special woman to marry me."

Mr. Hopewell's face softened slightly. "I pray that the owl will mean a more promising future for us both."

"Do you wish to hold the owl?"

"I cannot." The man with the gleaming eyes took a step back. "I can have no direct contact with the owl or the child it is to be given to. Even though the lives I hope to save in this time are no blood-kin of mine, the action taken today might alter the future of my relations. I want to avoid evidence of my involvement."

"Understood." John the Third removed the clockwork owl from the table, placed it carefully into a waiting wooden box. The box had been lined with black cloth, and the brass bird shone all the brighter when placed on the dark fabric. He laid Mr. Hopewell's calling card on top of the wind-up toy, and put the box's lid on. Lastly, he tied the box closed with a length of cord and tucked the scrap of paper with the delivery address beneath the cord's bow.

"I will be waiting on the steps of this house," he promised as he tapped the slip of paper on top of the wooden box, "at ten minutes before five this evening. And I will knock upon the door at exactly five o'clock as you have requested."

Mr. Hopewell nodded, slipped on his gloves, set his top hat on his head, and touched the hat's brim with a forefinger in a farewell gesture.

"Wait," said John. "Before your leave, I must ask—were you serious about killing me if I did not complete the owl by today?"

With a flourish worthy of a heroic novel, the man with the glittering eyes twisted then pulled upon the handle of his cane to reveal a wicked looking sword. "You shall never know," he responded as he returned the blade to the secret compartment in his cane and screwed the handle back in place. He strolled out the door without further comment.

John the Third looked up from his work table as a woman and boy entered his shop. The parts of a pocket watch and his tools were spread in front of him. He took off his magnifying eyepiece and nodded at the customer.

"May I help you?"

"I hope so," replied the woman as she held out a wooden box tied with a frayed cord. "I have a wind-up toy from my childhood that I would like to sell." She patted the shoulder of the boy. "My son, Henry, is much more interested in toy trains, and I thought I would use the money from this owl to add to his collection."

The clock maker took the familiar box with trembling hands, untied the cord, lifted the lid, and saw the clockwork owl he had made over twenty years before.

"Yes," he said. John cleared his throat. "Yes, I am interested in purchasing this owl. What are you asking for it."

The woman smiled, and named a more-than-reasonable price.

"But I must warn you," she added, "I think it might not be in perfect working order. "

The clock maker frowned. "What do you mean?"

"Years ago, it chirped. An awful noise, I must say. Loud enough to wake the dead." The woman adjusted the boy's jacket. "But it warned my family when some embers set the dining room rug ablaze. That silly little toy saved our home, and quite possibly my life."

John managed to reply, "The price is fair, even if it no longer makes noise."

He paid the woman the sum she had requested, and waved to her and Henry as they departed. Then, the faithful husband, father of four, and prosperous clock, watch, and wind-up toy maker went back to his storage room to locate an address in Boston.

*A*s the tall case clock in his bedroom struck nine, John the Third looked up from his pillow. A well-dressed man with gleaming gray eyes stood by his granddaughter at the side of his bed.

"Grandfather," said Elizabeth. "Someone to see you. A Mr. Hopewell who says you are old friends. Are you up to a visit?"

"Mr. Hopewell," said the old clock maker as he reached a heavily veined hand out to his visitor.

The man with the glinting eyes sat in a nearby chair, and grasped John's hand.

"Then, I will leave you two to chat about old times," said Elizabeth as she walked out of the bedroom, quietly closing the door behind her.

"I never thought to see you again," said John in a hoarse voice. "I met the girl to whom the clockwork owl was given. She came in the shop with her son, so I knew we had saved the lives in my time. But I have wondered all my life if we made a difference in your..."

A bout of coughing interrupted him.

Mr. Hopewell reached for the cup and pitcher on the bedside table and poured John a drink. He reached under the clock maker's head, lifted it slightly, and held the cup while John sipped some water.

"You did well. My sister and nephews are fine."

The clock maker relaxed into his pillow. "Who would have thought a wind-up toy could save lives, change the future, and bring me such happiness."

"It brought us both happiness, John the Third," responded Mr. Hopewell.

The clock maker closed his eyes for a moment. Then, he recalled one more query he wanted to make of his time-traveling customer, "Whatever became of the owl?"

Mr. Hopewell smiled and squeezed his bony hand. "I retrieved it, along with my journals, from the Boston law firm to which you mailed the owl. Since then, the journals have been destroyed. As for the owl automaton, it was donated to a museum. It is displayed for public viewing with a sign that reads: *Clockwork Owl. Late 1800s. Made by John the Third—Clock, watch, and toy maker.*"

The man with the gleaming eyes squeezed his hand one more time, stood, and stepped to the door. "So you are famous, John. Your name and work will live long after you and I are gone."

And as Mr. Hopewell bid farewell to Elizabeth and exited the fine home of John the Third's family, the old clock maker fell asleep for the last time dreaming of a shiny brass owl fluttering his wings, opening and closing his beak, blinking his eyes, and shuffling forward in a most unowl-like manner.

Pawprints of the Margay

*O*n *the morning after the Singing Fish Moon, a thunder-*clap caused Alazne, Diviner of the Kemen, to look up from spreading bufflehead guano on her vegetable garden. In the pale green sky, she saw a shimmering ship sail through the clouds, skim across the Rio Izar, and settle on the shores of Curro Seina. The Diviner set aside the manure and plunged her hands into a bucket of water. She instructed her stunned apprentice, Damita, to do the same. After both women had wiped their hands on a drying rag, Alazne grabbed her walking stick and bag of magics.

"We must hurry, child" the Diviner said as she headed towards the shore.

"Walk slower, Alazne," begged her apprentice.

The Diviner slackened her pace, aware that her apprentice's leg malformation was more severe than her own. "We need to reach the shore as soon as possible. The people will want to know what to make of this event."

Damita limp-jogged until she caught up with Alazne. "What will you tell them?"

"Whatever the Ancestors of the Kemen want me to tell their children."

Damita nodded and recited Alazne's mantra: "The Ancestors have the answers. We just need to listen for their voices."

Alazne smiled. She was proud her apprentice understood that this day, like all the ones before, contained a lesson. Damita was a good student. And an old Diviner needed a good student.

Alazne pursed her lips as they hastened through the narrow streets of Curro Seina. The pawprints of the Margay had foretold of strange visitors, but she had expected a ship upon the waters, not a ship on the wind. Though Alazne's skills were fading, Damita was not ready to make the transformation. Alazne must continue to serve the Ancestors and the Kemen for a little longer.

"Alazne. Alazne and Damita. The Diviners are here." The people of Curro Seina shouted as the women arrived and stood before the massive sky ship.

"Took you long enough, Diviner," said Platon. He scowled. "What sort of ship is this? What does it want?" The Head of the Council struck his spear upon the ground for emphasis. The owl feathers, shells, and leather thongs dangling from the shaft near the spearhead clattered.

Alazne withdrew a large moonstone from her bag, held it above her head, and called out, "Wise Ancestors of the Kemen, give us a sign. Help us understand this ship that sails upon the winds."

The villagers became quiet. The seabirds screeched. The waves sloshed upon the shore. As Alazne lowered the moonstone, a grinding noise came from within the sky ship. Most of the people of Curro Seina backed away from the metal hull. Platon and the rest of the warriors stepped forward, raised their shields, and began rhythmically striking their spears on the ground.

Alazne hobbled to stand in front of the warriors. She heard Damita breathing heavily at her side. She glanced in her apprentice's direction. Damita's lower lip was quivering, but the young woman stood shoulders back, chin lifted. The Diviner smiled, nodded. Damita would do.

Alazne turned her attention back to the sky ship. It towered above her, but she felt no fear. Sure in the power of the Ancestors and the truth of the Margay, she slipped the moonstone back into her bag and waited for the visitors to reveal themselves.

More grinding, clangs, and whirring sounds emanated from the sky ship. A portion of the bow split open. A silver walkway folded out and two white creatures with domed heads ambled down the ramp towards the people of Curro Seina. Many of the villagers screamed, ran back to their houses. Platon and the warriors held their spears and shields in the defensive position. Alazne, followed by a quaking Damita, shuffled forward.

"The Kemen, children of the Rio Izar greet you and offer you the hospitality of our Ancestors."

The white creatures talked among themselves using a language foreign to Alazne. The creatures fumbled with buttons at their necks, then lifted their domed heads off. The warriors pressed closer to Alazne and her apprentice. The Diviner raised her right hand and gestured for them to wait.

Beneath the domed shells, Alazne saw the creatures from the sky ship were humans like the Kemen. Their skin was pale and their hair the color of drying grain. Still, they were just a man and a woman.

One of the sky-people adjusted his necklace, then spoke. This time, he spoke in words the Kemen could understand. "Honorable Kemen, we come as friends. We come to learn more about the ways of the people of Rio Izar."

Platon stepped forward beside the Diviner and her apprentice. "I am Platon, Head of the Council of Curro Seina. How do we know you speak the truth?"

The sky-man touched a silver ear cuff, adjusted his necklace again. "I am Steen, and I offer you my word as a member of the League of Aboriginal Anthropologists."

Platon glanced at Alazne. She shrugged her shoulders.

"And I offer you this token of our friendship." Sky-man Steen held a shiny metal knife out to Platon. The sunlight reflected off of its blade.

"Ah." Platon reached out, took the proffered weapon. He examined its bejeweled handle. "Welcome, Steen. You must come to my house and be my guest."

Alazne cleared her throat.

Platon frowned, then pointed to the women. "Steen, this is our Diviner, Alazne, and her apprentice, Damita."

"Madam, I am honored to meet you."

Alazne tilted her head. She was not sure she was honored to meet Steen.

"And this is my associate, Haldis." Sky-woman Haldis touched her necklace and ear cuff, stepped forward, and smiled at the Diviner.

Alazne saw her eyes were the color of the Rio Izar on a clear day.

"Diviner Alazne, Apprentice Damita, I offer you small gifts to show my friendship." Sky-woman Haldis opened her hands to reveal two crystals that glowed amber in the daylight—the amber of Margay fur.

"These are generous gifts, suitable for a Diviner. We accept them and invite you to visit our home, Haldis." Alazne nudged Damita. The young woman grabbed the crystals, slid them into her bag. The Diviner studied the sky-woman's eyes. "Welcome, Haldis, to Curro Seina, first village of the Kemen."

Sky-woman Haldis smiled again, nodded at the Diviner and her apprentice. The two sky-people placed their domed head shells on the ramp, which drew them into the belly of the ship. They removed their bulky white clothing to reveal another set of clothes. This set of clothes was dark blue. The color reminded Alazne of the indigo dye used to design the beautiful fabrics of Kemen robes and tunics. The sky-people put their white clothing onto the ramp, and the suits quickly disappeared into the ship's belly.

"Come, both of you," urged Platon. "We will prepare a feast, and you must speak to the Council of the Wise."

"We will gladly tell you about our world, but more importantly, we have come to learn about the Kemen," answered a grinning Steen.

Alazne studied Steen's parted lips and white teeth. This was not the smile of a child, she decided. It was the sneer of a wolf.

The sky-people, Platon, the warriors, and the Diviner and her apprentice paraded through the stony lanes of Curro Seina. Villagers peeped from the windows of their bisque colored houses. Some brave villagers stood on the rock steps of their dwellings or beside the mud and straw granaries that out-numbered the homes four to one.

Soon, the visitors and their hosts arrived at the village center. The sky-people paused to examine the adobe shelter. They seemed especially interested in the eight Ancestor Pillars that supported the thatched roof.

"Who are the Kemen carved into the wood?" Steen rubbed his hand over the polished teak wood. His stony eyes slid from one carving to the other.

"The Ancestors. Each side of each pillar is a sacred Ancestor. For each Ancestor, there is a tale about the Kemen and their heritage. But these are not the only Ancestor carvings," bragged Platon with a wave of his hand.

"Really. You must show them all to me, and I must hear the tales that go with each figure."

"The Diviner is the storyteller. She can tell each of the Ancestor's tales and the history of the Kemen from the carvings."

Steen looked from Platon to Alazne. Alazne narrowed her eyes. She did not like Steen and his wolfish face. The Oracle had warned of a predator coming to devour the Kemen. Alazne thought Steen might be that predator. She had not decided yet about Haldis of the river eyes.

"How about it, Diviner? Tell us a tale."

"As you ask." Alazne motioned for everyone to find a seat either on the cool stone floor or on one of the wooden benches. Many of the people of Curro Seina had gathered outside the open-sided village center. They, too, found a comfortable place to rest and listen as the Diviner told an Ancestor tale.

"The Ancestors descended from the cliffs on steps they had chiseled from the orange rocks of Raul Escarpment. They brought with them their goats, their sheep, their chickens, and donkeys. Trella, the first Diviner, advised the Ancestors on where to build the paths, how to chock the boulders to make the way safe. Nightly, Trella visited the plateau on top of Raul Escarpment with questions for the Margay. Nightly, Trella traced the signs and symbols of the Kemen in the soil, then she placed a small food offering in the middle of the question wheel."

Alazne paused. She heard the villagers humming. Some were gently slapping their thighs with the palms of their hands.

"Nightly, Trella knelt beside the question wheel beneath the blanket of stars and waited. Each night, the amber furred Margay leaped from his tree bed. Each night, the golden eyed Margay walked on silent paws. Each night, the long tailed Margay studied the tracings and danced the answers to the questions of the Kemen. For the Margay are the Oracles, the Seers of things to come."

Alazne paused again. The villagers, warriors, and elders were swaying. The rhythm of their slapping had reached a frenzied pace, though their humming remained as muted as the buzz of sand flies.

"One starless night, after the Margay had danced the answers to the questions of the Kemen, the sacred cat turned to Trella. It spoke to her in the spirit voice of magic things. The Margay demanded a payment for its prophecies, demanded a payment for allowing the Diviner to interpret its pawprints. Trella bowed her head and offered her body to the Margay as payment. The sacred cat danced around Trella three times. As the Margay passed by her legs for the third time, it slashed her thigh and bit her flesh."

The people of Curro Seina clapped three times. Moaned. Then, they were silent.

"This satisfied the Margay, who licked the wound, then danced away into the darkness of a thorn thicket. The maimed Trella began to read the footsteps of the Oracle. The Margay promised the Kemen a future of good health and many descendants, but only if they lived by the traditions of their forefathers. The Oracle promised wells that provided water and fields that yielded plentiful harvests in the rugged land of Curro Seina, but only if they observed the sacred rituals. And the Oracle promised that the Kemen would live on the shores of the Rio Izar until Raul Escarpment was whittled down to a plain if they kept their ways pure, unspoiled by the ways of outsiders."

The humming resumed. Alazne turned to face Steen and Haldis. They were the only people not swaying, humming, and slapping their thighs. "And so from the time of Trella to this day, the Kemen have kept to themselves, honoring their Ancestors, observing the sacred rituals, and shunning the world beyond the shores of the Rio Izar. And all Diviners, marked at birth by the Margay with an ill-formed leg, are duty bound to uphold the ways of the Kemen and protect the people from evil."

"Look!" said Alazne pointing to the carved figure of an old woman staring from the teak column directly in front of Steen. "Look! For even now, Trella waits to curse those who would dishonor the old ways."

Steen curled his lips and showed his too white teeth. "Well, that was certainly entertaining. We will have to hear more tales from the Diviner another time. But now, I will tell you about the sky ship and the worlds of my people."

Platon, the Council members, and many of the villagers listened to Steen tell of the sky ship that soared not only in the clouds above Raul Escarpment, Curro Seina, and the Rio Izar—but even among the stars that were sewn in the night sky by the First Ancestor. Steen explained the magic necklaces and ear cuffs that talked in both the language of the sky-people and the language of the Kemen. He promised wondrous gifts to the villagers in exchange for a few pieces of Kemen Ancestor carving.

"We cannot trade away our carvings" warned Alazne. "It is taboo."

"Sit down, Diviner," Platon ordered. "In the village center, at the Council of the Wise, I am the voice of the people of Curro Seina. And I want to hear what Steen has to say."

"Come, Damita, we will leave the Council of the Greedy to their work."

The Diviner Alazne and her apprentice limped away. Most of the Council members whistled at their backs as they left the village center. But the Diviner and her apprentice did not go far. They slipped behind a granary, then made their way back to the village center. Though hidden, they saw and heard all.

As they watched, Steen sent Haldis back to their ship for gifts while he continued to tell of the helpful things the sky-people would give the Kemen in exchange for the carvings. When Haldis returned, the sky-people gave each elder and villager a package of fire-starters.

"These are matches," Steen said. "With these, it is easy to start a fire even when the coals have gone cold." Steen demonstrated how to ignite the fire-starters. The people of Curro Seina gasped when fire sprang from the little sticks, then hurried to their homes to try the matches.

After eating dinner with Platon and the Council of the Wise, Steen and Haldis returned to their ship. They moved slowly, burdened by the weight of the shields, spears, and masks that had been given to them in appreciation for the fire-starters.

Alazne and Damita watched from the shadows and followed the outsiders. They overheard Steen tell Haldis, "This is going to be easy. They are a naive lot."

"It is not right," Sky-woman Haldis replied. "We should not be disrupting the lives of the Kemen."

"My funding depends on something spectacular. And, dear Haldis, those ancestor carvings are just the ticket."

Alazne noticed the sky-woman flinch at the words: *dear Haldis*.

The sky-woman frowned. "I only agreed to come with you on this expedition because no one else was available. I am not comfortable with what you are doing here." Haldis glanced at Steen. "We don't need any other artifacts. These shields and masks are wonderful, and it is not taboo for us to take them."

"But not as wonderful as the carvings." Steen stepped in front of the sky-woman. "You are nothing more than a researcher. It is is best to leave field decisions to those with experience."

Haldis paused, and looked him in his rock-gray eyes. "This might be my first field expedition, but I know the rules. And you are breaking them. The Kemen trust you. Your unscrupulous behavior could endanger both their culture and future relations with them."

"Do not go soft on me," warned the sky-man. "I *will* get some of those carvings, and I would hate to think you were working against me."

Haldis started to respond, but instead shook her head, lowered her gaze, and resumed walking. Without further conversation, the sky-people boarded their boat and closed its metal hull.

"We must warn the elders," Damita whispered as they trudged back to their house on the outskirts of Curro Seina.

"I have already warned them."

"We must do something."

The Diviner patted her apprentice's hand. "We will be like the rock viper who waits in the shade of a crevice until the foolish mouse wanders by and is caught unawares."

"I hope Steen does not know the fable of the mouse and the rock viper."

Alazne chuckled. "I do not think he would recognize the rattle of a rock viper. The sound of profit is the only sound he hears."

*I*n the predawn twilight as the cliff owls swooped back to their holes, Alazne listened to the rhythm of the women of Curro Seina pounding millet and chopping firewood. She witnessed them caring for their children, drawing water from the village wells, and balancing the pottery water jugs on top of their heads for the journey back to their houses. The Diviner saw the men of Curro Seina carrying their hoes to the fields and heard their deep voices chanting the working tunes of the Kemen. The cadence of the teamwork songs and the timeless routine of the daily chores reaffirmed what she already knew. Alazne rubbed her thigh. Hidden beneath her skirt and tunic was the mark of the Margay: the four parallel blue lines tattooed into her flesh. And as the Diviner studied her deeply etched palms, she formulated a plan.

*A**t sunrise, Damita brought the Diviner her morning meal.** *After the ritual of thanks, Alazne and her apprentice each ate a bowl of millet porridge sweetened with thornberries.

"Today, you will act as Diviner," said Alazne as she finished her porridge.

Damita furrowed her brow. "I am not sure I am ready. What if I make a mistake?"

Alazne pointed to the carved turtle amulet dangling between her breasts. "You are like the ancient tortoise, slow and steady and careful. You are ready."

Damita nodded, gathered their dirty bowls and spoons. She rinsed and stacked them. As the women checked the contents of their magic bags, Fraco the beer brewer knocked on the side of their house.

"Diviner, I have come to ask a question of the Margay."

Alazne and Damita limped onto their stone porch.

"Today, Damita will be the Diviner. Today, you must talk with her about your questions," said Alazne.

The beer brewer looked from old woman to young woman. He nodded. "Damita, Diviner of the Kemen, I offer you these five eggs, three bonefish, and a jar of beer. I beseech you to take my questions to the Oracle."

"Fraco, your Ancestors are Kemen, you are Kemen, and your children until the last generation will be Kemen. What do you ask of the Oracle?" droned Damita.

"Should I trade one of my carved granary doors to the sky-people for better tools, sturdier pans, and more matches?"

"Any other questions for the Margay?"

"Platon's son wants to marry my youngest daughter, but her older sisters are not yet married. Do I grant the Council Head's request or insist he help me find husbands for my two older daughters first?"

"I will consult with the Oracle in two nights. Return on the third day, and I will have your answers." The beer brewer bowed his head, turned, and walked back to his brewery.

"Good job. I could not have done better."

Damita seemed to glow as her teacher praised her performance.

"It is a shame that a man with such a respectful manner and sincere wish to do what is right is not on the Council of the Wise," observed Alazne. "Of course, when a new council is selected in the autumn, perhaps someone will put forth his name."

"Maybe we could..." began Damita.

But the women did not have time to discuss Fraco the beer brewer's good qualities or his questions for the Margay. A young boy ran into their yard jabbering about his mother.

"Shush, young one. Now, slowly tell Diviner Damita what is wrong," urged Alazne.

The boy took several breaths. "My mother's baby is coming. She calls for the Diviner to bring her magics. She calls for the Diviner to deliver her in the blessed way."

"Who is your mother?" Damita asked the boy.

"Leya, daughter of the potter."

"Run home. We will be there as soon as we gather the necessary magics." Damita turned to go in the house, then stopped when she saw Alazne smiling.

"Daughter of my heart, you are indeed ready to become a Diviner. When we visit the Margay in two nights' time, you will make the transformation and take your place as the Diviner of Curro Seina."

"But what of you, Alazne?"

"I will be your adviser, but you will be the chief Diviner."

Damita bowed her head. "Mother of my heart, you will always be the wiser one. I thank you for your patience, for your lessons, and for the promise of your advice. I will always be your grateful daughter."

Alazne hugged Damita. "We had better get to the house of Leya, daughter of the potter, if we are to welcome the newest Kemen of Curro Seina."

The women scurried down the lane to the house of Leya. Damita used the power of the bloodstone and the massage techniques of the Ancestors to help the small-hipped Leya deliver a healthy son. The grateful potter gifted them with two beautiful water jugs. Leya's husband gave them each five ground-pears in payment. And because they had business with the Council of the Wise, Leya's older son agreed to carry the jugs and fruit to the Diviners' house for the women.

As Alazne and Damita walked through the streets of Curro Seina towards the village center, the old Diviner casually mentioned to Damita that both the potter and Leya's husband would make excellent additions to the Council of the Wise.

"I agree," the younger woman responded. "If either one of them was selected to replace Platon, I think even the Ancestors would smile."

They both laughed, but became silent when they saw Steen talking to the Kemen. Then, they saw Haldis, who was using a string of light to measure the houses, granaries, and carved teak doors. When she turned around, the Diviners nodded at the sky-woman.

"Alazne, Damita, good to see you." Haldis motioned for the Diviners to come closer. "We are measuring your buildings and taking pictures. Would you like to see?"

Damita turned her head towards Alazne. Alazne remained silent. "Yes, we would like to know what the sky-people are doing."

Haldis demonstrated the device that measured the size and shape of the dwellings.

"We do much the same thing with measuring string," said Damita.

Haldis showed how she touched buttons and a picture-box painted a picture of what it saw on a tiny plate.

"We paint our pictures on wooden planks, animal skins, and on sacred cliff rocks," the younger Kemen woman told the anthropologist.

Haldis studied the quiet Alazne. "You are not speaking today. Is there something wrong?"

The old woman shook her head. "Today, Damita is the Diviner. She has said the right things. But I do have a question."

The sky-woman leaned closer, tapped her ear cuff, and studied Alazne's mouth as it formed the words.

"After you trade for some of the granary doors, will you go away, never to sail into Curro Seina again? Or will more of your kind return for the Ancestor carvings of the Kemen?"

Wrinkles appeared between the river blue eyes of the sky-woman. "I do not know. Steen is in charge, and he is determined to bring news of the Kemen to the League's attention."

"Then, more sky-people will follow you. You can say it to us, for we are Diviners, and the Oracle will tell us anyway when we visit."

Haldis sighed, lifted her hands, then let them fall. "I will not lie to you, Alazne. More anthropologists are sure to follow when they see the carvings. It is rare to find such treasures in perfect condition. The sky-people will come not to change your ways, but to understand them."

"Haldis, I think you know as we do that by coming to observe the old ways, the observers will bring new ways. The Ancestors will soon be dishonored and forgotten. How can the children of a Kemen family remember the tales of their bloodline when the carvings are gone and the elders die?"

"I am sorry. There is nothing I can do to prevent more anthropologists from coming."

"Is there not something?" asked Alazne.

Haldis did not answer. Instead, she looked down at the measuring light in her hand.

"When are you to trade for the granary doors?" inquired Damita.

The sky-woman raised her head and responded, "As soon as the men of each family are able to construct a crude replacement. I imagine we'll begin to acquire some of the carved doors tomorrow."

"Crude replacement?" Alazne clucked her tongue. "You mean some kindling lashed together to seal the granaries. There will be no Ancestors protecting the food-stores from thieves, no sacred animals chasing away disease and evil spirits. This will be the death of the Kemen."

"I cannot change what is happening." Alazne noticed there were tears in the eyes of the sky-woman. "Steen is in charge. I am only his associate on this expedition. My vote to leave the Kemen, the children of the Rio Izar, as we found them does not count."

"There is always a way," said the old Diviner before she and Damita hurried to the village center.

As they traversed the well-worn lanes to the meeting place of the Council of the Wise, they saw men eagerly at work on new granary doors.

"I do not think we can stop this from happening, Alazne."

"We will see."

The women arrived at the village center. Platon and several of the other elders were lounging in the cool shade of the center's thatched roof. A scrawny dog yapped at the Diviners as they entered the meeting place. "We have come to ask you to reconsider allowing the villagers to trade carved granary doors to the sky-people," said Alazne.

Platon raised his eyebrows. "When I need the spiritual advice of a Diviner, I will ask for it. The Council has voted. We have decided that each family will be allowed to trade one granary door to the outsiders. Raul Escarpment will not fall into the Rio Izar because we have traded away one fourth of the granary doors. We have instructed the people to select the oldest door. Those Ancestors have drifted the greatest distance into the world of the dead. It is a wise compromise."

The rest of the elders relaxing in the village center mumbled their agreement.

"Platon, you are a foolish man. The sky-man will not be satisfied with a few granary doors. Steen sees treasure to be had, and he will find a way to have it all. If not tomorrow, then by the Storm Moon, or by the Moon of the Full Baskets. Only the Margay knows the exact date, but everyone here knows in their heart that Steen will return for more carvings."

Platon stepped closer to Alazne, glared down into her wrinkled face. "Because you're a Diviner, because you are old and deserve some consideration, I will not strike you. But if you ever call me a fool again, I will send you sprawling in the dust. Do you understand, Alazne?"

"Too well, Platon. Too well." The Diviner looked into the eyes of each of the elders in the village center. "Remember this day, Council members, for you have invited evil into the village of Curro Seina. The Ancestors and the Oracle will have their say, even if you do not ask their opinion."

Alazne rummaged through her bag of magics, withdrew her moonstone, and dropped it on the floor. The seeing stone shattered. Legend promised all who had witnessed the destruction of the talisman were now cursed, save the Diviners. The elders leapt to their feet, yelling and making warding signs. Alazne and Damita limped away from the men, refusing to acknowledge their shouts.

That afternoon, several village families visited the House of the Diviners. Each brought their offerings of food, drink, and other goods. Damita listened to their questions, promised an answer from the Oracle. Alazne perched nearby on the Diviner's ceremonial chair. She remained silent.

As the women sat beside the cooking fire, watching the first stars flicker in the evening heavens, Damita turned to Alazne. "It has been bothering me all day. Why did you destroy the moonstone? Where will we find a replacement?"

"The Ancestors demanded it," stated the older Diviner. "But do not worry, daughter. Tomorrow, I will take you to the forbidden place where the magic stones of the Ancestors are hidden. You need to visit it anyway, so you may show your apprentice. And someday, she will show her apprentice."

Damita nodded as they watched the crescent moon lift from the Rio Izar like a dipper from a water bucket.

*T*he next morning, as the Diviners made the preparations for their journey to the forbidden place and to the Haunt of the Margay; they heard someone knocking on the door.

"Hello. Alazne? Damita? Are you there?" Sky-woman Haldis stood on their porch. The hot sun reflecting off the Rio Izar and the adobe buildings had reddened her white skin.

"I have been waiting for you," said Alazne. Damita opened her mouth to speak, but Alazne signaled her apprentice to be still. "You, sky-woman Haldis, have respect for tradition and are humble in the presence of the Ancestors. You have come to help us protect the ways of the Kemen."

"Yes," answered Haldis. "Though I break the laws of the sky-people, I will protect the Kemen." Sky-woman Haldis rubbed her brow with her right hand, then continued, "There *is* something I can do, but it is as wrong as tricking you out of your carvings and opening the door for change. Perhaps, it is even more wrong."

"Still, you are willing to do what is necessary?"

"Yes," sighed the sky-woman. "Steen is violating League rules. But by the time I can bring a complaint to our superiors, it will be too late for the Kemen."

Alazne bowed her head, then lifted her chin and stared into the river eyes of Haldis. "Then, as Diviner of the Kemen, keeper of the Ancestral secrets, and servant of the Oracle—I invite you, Sky-woman Haldis to be Assistant to the Diviner."

Alazne bent down, pinched a bit of dirt between her fingers. "Never will you take your place as Diviner since you are not Kemen, but you will ever be welcome in this House." Alazne pressed the dirt against the sky-woman's forehead. "In time, you'll become knowledgeable in the sacred rituals. When I am called to be with the Ancestors, you will keep Damita company and help her perform the duties of Diviner. Upon your death, you will be carried through the streets of Curro Seina as an honored member of the village."

Alazne placed one of her hands on either side of the face of Haldis. "Will you swear to serve the Kemen and the Oracle and keep secret their rituals and sacred traditions?"

"Yes," the sky-woman whispered.

"Will you turn your back on Steen and the sky-people from this day forward, and ever put the Kemen and the Oracle first?

Haldis hesitated, chewed on her lower lip. Then, she closed her eyes and nodded, yes.

"Will you learn the language of the people of Curro Seina so the magic necklace and ear cuff may be cast aside?"

"Yes." There were tears running down the reddened skin of Haldis. "I will do what is necessary to protect the ways of the Kemen."

"So the Oracle foresaw. So it will be."

Alazne took Haldis's hand, placed it in the hand of Damita. "Diviner, meet your Assistant. Assistant, meet your Diviner. Damita, meet the sister of your heart. Haldis, meet the sister of your heart." Alazne kissed each woman on her right cheek. "Daughters of my heart, I need your strength for what is to come."

"I will do what I can, Diviner," said Haldis the Assistant.

"As will I," said Damita.

"Good. For now, we must search out the forbidden place."

*T*he three women talked quietly as they trudged to the foot of Raul Escarpment. Each carried a woven bag. Haldis was healthy and strong, so she carried the heaviest sack. Alazne and Damita limped under the lesser weight of their bags.

As they began the ascent on the well-worn steps to the burial caves of the Kemen, they passed a wayside relic carved in the shape of leaping jackal.

"The Watchstone warns of death to those who enter the Caves of the Dead," said Alazne. "But we'll be safe—for we have come to help the Kemen, not to grave rob."

The younger women climbed the stairs as far away from the Watchstone as possible. The gaping mouth of the growling beast still jutted over their heads. Alazne observed Damita and Haldis. Wide-eyed, they glanced at each other and seemed to take comfort in the fact that they were both frightened.

The old Diviner raised her hand as the women came to a fork in the path.

"To the right there are nine Caves of the Dead. Those caves are for the villagers. In each of the Caves of the Kemen are many bones—but there is room for many more. Today, we will be going left." Alazne gestured to walk on the path that wound its way up the left side of the cliff.

A short time later, they stood at the mouth of the first burial cave. Above the entrance hung a grimacing mask and on either side, two towering pillars of coati skulls leered at the Diviners and their Assistant.

The young women hesitated at the cave entrance. "How much farther do we have to go?" asked Damita in a small voice.

"We must go through the Cave of the Wise, up more steps, through another cave, up more steps, and into the third cave. That is where we will find what we seek."

Damita and Haldis held hands as they entered the first Cave of the Dead, the final resting place of the Council members. On either side of the path, thousands of skeletons were stacked like firewood. Faded bits of indigo fabric fluttered from exposed ribs. The rustling of small creatures scuttling among the bones and the squeaks and flutterings of a huge colony of bats could be heard.

"Look," said Alazne as she pointed to rows of carved figures and a pile of pottery shards. "The funeral statuettes of the dead and the burial objects of remembrance."

The younger women followed the old Diviner without comment up the next set of stairs. These steps, too, were shiny from the thousands of Kemen who had trudged upon them on their funeral journeys. When they entered the next Cave of the Dead, the wind howled.

"It sounds like village women grieving," murmured Damita.

"As it should, for this if the Cave of the Young. Here is where mothers bury their children and the babies who do not live through the birthing."

Damita and Haldis held even tighter to each other's hands as they wended their way through the stacks of small skeletons. Diviner Alazne glanced at the tiny exposed arms. She thought they looked like thin stems that ended in delicate flower blossoms. Instead of statuettes at the back of this cave, there were rows of children's toys and shell debris. She saw the younger women blink as they moved into the sunshine again.

"This is the last set of steps for us to climb today—but be careful, a rock slide knocked away part of the path. The men have masoned new steps on the cliff side, but they are not as wide as the rest of the trail."

The three women climbed the stairs and stood panting in front of the third Cave of the Dead. On either side of its entrance, carved crocodiles crept up the overarching walls. In the center of the archway, there was a bas-relief of a cat.

"This is the Cave of the Diviners, the burial chamber of the servants of the Margay. This is where I will be carried. This is where each of you will be carried by the young men of Curro Seina when the Ancestors call you."

"It is a much smaller cave," ventured Haldis.

The old woman nodded. "There have been many Diviners, but only one Diviner for a village full of Kemen." Alazne plucked an oil lamp from a shelf chiseled into the side of the cave wall, walked off the path, and picked her way through the skulls and leg bones. "Over here," she called to the younger women.

A large colony of cave owls watched the progress of the trio. Their over-sized eyes reflected the light from the the lamp. And as Haldis and Damita tiptoed through the scattered remains and followed Alazne into a narrow passage that led deeper into the cliff face, the owls clicked their talons against rock and hooted in soft, low voices.

No one spoke to the night birds. Instead, the three women roamed the secret maze of passageways that honeycombed the cliff.

"Ah, here is what we came for," sighed Alazne as she lifted her oil lamp. Hundreds of semiprecious stones glittered in the light cast by the lamp. "We must find two moonstones, a bloodstone, three pieces of lapis lazuli, and two polished cat's-eyes," she said.

The women searched through the rocks until they had found the needed magic stones. Alazne chanted a prayer of thanksgiving and led Haldis and Damita back through the passageways to the main burial cave. She signaled for the younger women to remain silent, then hurried them past the owl colony and to the cave entrance.

"Turn around and back out of the cave so the spirits of the dead do not follow us."

The younger women obeyed her order. The trio repeated the ritual at the entrance to the Cave of Young and at the first Cave of the Wise. Though near exhaustion, Alazne urged Damita and Haldis to scramble down the Raul Escarpment steps and paths. When they had finally reached the scrub lands and forests of Curro Seina, the old Diviner collapsed in the shade of a pecan tree.

"Now, we rest."

"Why did we have to rush?" inquired Haldis.

"The spirits of the dead and things of dark magic will try to ride the backs of the living into the valley. Then, they will sicken the livestock and poison the water," answered Damita.

Alazne nodded. "Now, we must eat before we go to the Haunt of the Margay," said the old Diviner.

"I am starved," said Haldis. "But I forgot how hungry I was when we were in the caves. I do not think I could find the chamber with the sacred stones again. The passageway seemed to cross back over itself several times."

"I have studied the way, but I had never been to the Caves of the Dead until today," said Damita between mouthfuls of ground-pear. "I think I could find it again, but I would be frightened to go alone."

"You will not be alone. I will go with you next time, too," promised Haldis.

The old Diviner remained quiet and smiled at the friendship developing between the younger women.

After the three women ate and drank their fill, they rested for another hour in the shade of the pecan tree. Alazne told them about the Margay—new tales to Haldis, familiar ones to Damita.

"During the day, the Margay are tree dwellers. They are tucked away in the branches, feasting on slow birds and lizards. At night, they walk headfirst down their tree and search the ground for wood-rats and rabbits."

"Headfirst? How is that possible?" asked Haldis.

"Shush," hissed Damita. "Let her finish the story."

The old Diviner patted the knees of the younger women. "It is alright, Damita. Haldis is just curious."

Damita sighed. "The Margay have flexible legs." She held up her hands, fingers curled. "They also have sharp claws."

Alazne patted their knees again, continued. "In the olden times, before the Kemen descended Raul Escarpment to Curro Seina, the first Diviner discovered one of the sacred Haunts of the Margay. There, she learned to draw the question wheel and interpret the pawprints of the Oracle. There, she saw the amber furred Margay up close. Saw its underbelly that glowed white as the spirits. Saw the dark eyes marking the fur of its back and flanks. Saw the striped tail sway like the Kemen when the old stories are told. And there, she struck a deal with the Oracle."

Alazne stopped talking, stood, and picked up her bag.

"What about the rest of the story?" asked Haldis as she scrambled to her feet.

"We will live the rest of the story tonight," replied the old Diviner. Without another word, Alazne turned and began the trek to the Haunt of the Margay.

The three women traveled through scrub and forest until they reached a secluded clearing. In the center of the clearing, there was a large sandy area. Alazne gestured to Damita, who withdrew a reddish powder from her bag of magics. The young Diviner circled the sandy area three times softly chanting and scattering the blood colored dust.

"Now, we must draw the question wheel," said Alazne.

Haldis and Alazne watched as Damita drew the symbols and signs that asked the questions of the Oracle that had been posed earlier in the week to the Diviners. Carefully, she placed a food offering for the Margay in the center of each question. When the question wheel was complete, Damita knelt beside the sandy etching and raised her hands to the emerging stars.

"Honorable Margay, Oracle of the Kemen, it is I, Damita of Curro Seina, daughter of the Rio Izar. I beg you to visit our question circle. My Ancestors are the Kemen who climbed down Raul Escarpment in the long ago days. The ancient mother of my heart is your servant, Trella, the First Diviner. Like Trella and all the Diviners before me, I honor you and humbly ask for you to answer our questions. Amber Margay, come dance the future of the Kemen."

"Daughter, you must lay beside the circle tonight," said Alazne. "If the Margay accepts you as his interpreter, I will mark you with the indigo tattoo of a Diviner."

Damita lifted her face, looked at the old Diviner. She nodded her assent and lay on her belly by the question circle. Moments later, the Margay slipped out of the trees, pranced over to the prone woman. The wildcat sniffed Damita, then raised his muzzle to inspect Alazne and Haldis. He seemed satisfied that they posed no threat. The Margay leapt to the center of the circle. He sniffed and pawed and danced and gobbled the tasty offerings.

When the food was gone, the Oracle whirled around, danced back to the prostrate woman. He prodded her with his paw but did not scratch Damita. The Margay stared once again at the old Diviner. He opened his mouth, seemed to smile, then growled a blood curdling cry. Before the women could speak, the Oracle vanished into the shadows.

"Read the pawprints of the Margay, Damita, then I will tattoo you with the marks of a true Diviner. The Oracle approved of you. The people of Curro Seina will be able to ask the wise Margay questions for many more years to come."

While Damita studied the pawprints of the Margay, Alazne aided by Haldis prepared the tattooing materials. When she had learned all she could learn from the Oracle, Damita once again lay on her belly. Haldis held her hand as the old Diviner pushed the blue dye into her thigh in four parallel lines. When the tattoo was complete, Alazne helped Damita to her feet.

"Blessings of the Ancestors upon you Diviner and," Alazne turned to Haldis, "blessings on you Diviner's Assistant. To you two, I give the future of the Kemen, for this night I will commit sacrilege in the name of the Ancestors."

"What do you mean?" asked Haldis.

Alazne drew three daggers from her bag. She handed one to each of the younger women.

"We are going to desecrate the Ancestor carvings. We will damage the granary doors just enough, so they are no longer perfect. They will not be as desirable to Steen. Should other sky-people come, they, too, will find them damaged and covet them less. You will both help me, but in the morning when the crime is discovered—I will take credit for the offense."

"They will kill you," warned Damita.

"Yes," answered the old Diviner. "But you and Haldis can carry on the traditions. I am old, tired. When last I read the pawprints of the Margay, they told me I must make a sacrifice to save the Kemen. And that is what I'm going to do."

"Is there no other way?"

Alazne shook her head. "But I am not the only one to make a sacrifice." The older woman turned towards Haldis. "You must destroy the sky ship and the outsider who would change the people of the Rio Izar."

"I know," whispered Steen's former associate. "I knew when I came to the House of the Diviners this morning."

"I am sorry, Haldis. There is no other way to save the Kemen." Alazne patted the shoulder of former sky-woman. "Come, we need to hurry.

The trio walked quickly back to Curro Seina. They gouged and hacked and scraped all of the carved granary doors in the village. If the dogs started to bark, the women tossed the mongrels food scraps to silence them. The stars were fading and the people stirring when Alazne, Damita, and Haldis arrived at the village center. Here, Alazne took back the knives from the younger women and ordered them to leave the structure.

"Good-bye, Alazne. Good-bye," they cried and hugged the old Diviner.

"Daughters of my heart, be strong for each other. The Oracle asked, and I agreed to this path. No matter what happens, remember I was true to the traditions of the Ancestors."

"Come with me, Damita," urged Haldis. "We must go to my ship and sabotage it. Steen cannot be allowed to reach our home base or communicate any further with League members."

Though Alazne doubted the young Diviner understood what Haldis was about to do, Damita willingly followed the former sky-woman as she hurried out of the village center towards the sky ship. Alazne felt a terrible sadness as she watched the young women disappear around the corner of a granary.

*F*rom where she was bound to one of the Ancestor support columns, Alazne saw Damita and Haldis return to the village center later that morning accompanied by Steen. The young

Diviner and her new Assistant seemed confused when they saw the villagers of Curro Seina shouting and arguing among themselves.

"What is this all about?" asked sky-man Steen.

"The old Diviner has gone mad," answered Council Head Platon, who was attempting to calm the crowd. "Alazne has damaged all the granary doors in Curro Seina and even defaced the sacred Ancestors on the columns of the village center."

Steen surveyed the angry crowd, rubbed his pale jaw. "I have come to say farewell to the Kemen of Curro Seina," he shouted to the crowd.

The villagers grew quiet.

"I thank you for the granary doors, spears, shields, and masks. I will treasure them always. As a gesture of my friendship, my associate Haldis will be staying with the Diviner Damita. Haldis will learn more about the Kemen by living among you—so upon my return, we can share even more wonders from the sky ship with the children of the Rio Izar."

Steen waved to the villagers, shook Platon's hand, clapped Haldis on the back, and jogged down the stony lane to his waiting vessel.

Platon watched the sky-man vanish behind the angry throng. "People of Curro Seina, the Council of the Wise has only one punishment for such blasphemy. To make sure our judgment is fair, we will ask the accused to speak." The Head of the Council turned to Alazne. "What say you, Diviner, to the charge that you deliberately damaged the carvings of the Ancestors?"

Alazne lifted her head, slowly scanned the villagers. When she spotted Damita and Haldis, she paused, then looked at the rest of the crowd. "I took my knife and marred the carvings of the Ancestors to prevent the Kemen from trading away their heritage."

Some in the crowd grumbled.

"You leave the Council little choice in the punishment if you cannot come up with a better excuse than that, Diviner." Platon said. A few villagers clenched and unclenched their fists. Some whistled. Most shook their heads and muttered their disagreement with Platon's words.

"I read the pawprints of the Margay. They told me to desecrate the carvings of the Ancestors in order to save the traditions of the Kemen. They told me Steen would be punished for interfering in the lives of the children of the Rio Izar. I will not apologize, and I ask for no mercy."

Enraged shouts erupted from a handful of the young men in the crowd. Alazne witnessed Damita and Haldis being jostled by the villagers. She observed Platon consulting with the rest of the Council of the Wise. Alazne, the old Diviner, took a deep breath as Platon faced the crowd once more and raised his hands.

"As Head of the Council of the Wise, it is my duty to sentence Diviner Alazne to death by stoning—the traditional punishment for the crime of sacrilege."

Ignoring shouts of protest, Platon signaled his warriors to escort the condemned woman to the shores of the Rio Izar. The Council followed the warriors and Alazne down the street. Behind her, Alazne knew Damita and Haldis would be swept along with the rest of the Kemen to the shores of the Rio Izar.

When the villagers reached the now vacant spot where the sky ship had been beached, some began to pick stones up from the ground. Platon raised his arms again. "As is the tradition in cases of sacrilege, the Diviner will cast the first stone. Damita, come forward."

From her place between two warriors, the condemned Alazne saw Damita look first at Platon and his Council, and then at Haldis.

"You must do this, just as I did what I had to do, just as Alazne did what she had to do," whispered Diviner's Assistant Haldis.

Damita stepped in front of the Kemen of Curro Seina, the children of the Rio Izar.

"Alazne, you have insulted the Ancestors, you have defaced their statues, you have dishonored the ways of the Kemen," shouted the new Diviner. Damita could not hide the tears streaming down her face. "Mother of my heart, it is I, Diviner of Curro Seina, who must cast the first stone."

As the smooth rock left Damita's hand, Alazne cried out, "Children of my heart, honor the ways of the Ancestors."

The rocks pelted the Diviner by the dozens. It was not long before Alazne felt her legs give out, and her knees sink to the sand. And as she saw the angriest villagers move in closer to finish the stoning, Alazne heard the voices of the Ancestors whispering a welcome.

When some of the villagers wandered away, Damita, Haldis, Fraco the beer brewer, the potter, the husband of Leya, and many of the other Kemen who recalled the many kindnesses of Alazne went to her broken body.

As was the tradition of the Kemen, the corpse of Alazne was placed on a board and carried head high through the village of Curro Seina. Damita, Haldis, and the other mourning women wailed behind the body. The funeral procession grew as it marched out of the village to Raul Escarpment. At the head of the procession, the bearers of Alazne's corpse struggled up the worn steps to the first Cave of the Dead. When they reached the entrance to the first cave, Damita and Haldis moved to the front of the procession.

Hand-in-hand, the Diviner and her Assistant led Alazne's funeral procession through the Cave of the Wise, up the second tier of steps, through the Cave of the Young, up the third tier of steps, to the entrance to the Cave of the Diviners. Only the corpse-bearers and the Diviner and her Assistant entered the third cave. There, under the watchful gaze of the owl colony, Alazne's body was placed beside the Diviners of old.

"Back away, friends of Alazne," ordered Damita as she, too, walked backwards out of the cave. "Sacred Oracle," shouted Damita. "We have brought your beloved servant, Alazne, home. She honored your wishes and was killed because she tried to save the ways of the Kemen by defacing the carvings of the Ancestors. We beseech you to welcome your Diviner home."

Then, Damita, Haldis, and all in the funeral procession heard a growl. They looked up and gasped—for there on the boulders above the entrance to the Cave of the Diviners stood a Margay. Its amber fur, marked with the eye-like patterns, shone in the morning sun.

There were gasps and screams from the villagers, for none but Damita and Haldis had ever seen the elusive wildcat before. The Diviner, her Assistant, and all of the people in the funeral procession fell to their knees, clasped their hands before their chests. They began to chant and sway.

As the religious fever of the villagers reached the point of ecstasy, a great explosion sounded in the clouds above Raul Escarpment. Pieces of the metal sky ship clattered onto the rocks around the funeral procession, rained on the fields of Curro Seina, and splashed in the Rio Izar.

In the stillness after the blast, the Margay looked down from its rocky perch. The sacred cat focused its eyes first on Damita, then on Haldis. The Margay screamed.

The Kemen hid their faces in their hands.

The Margay screamed again.

The Kemen wailed and begged for mercy.

The Margay, Oracle of the children of the Rio Izar, screamed a final time; then turned, raced up the cliff, and disappeared.

Owl Pellets

Owl pellets teach many lessons —
like who among us is squeamish
and who will sift
through owl vomit to locate
tiny bones.

Tiny bones teach many lessons —
like which creatures are cautious
and which will pay
for a moment of moonlight
with their quiet death.

Quiet death teaches many lessons —
like who will depart
without argument and who
will fight the inevitable
arrival of earthworms.

Earthworms teach many lessons —
like the equality
of owls, mice, and humans
when their flesh is a meal
that crumbles into soil.

Soil teaches many lessons —
like the work of earthworms is never done
and all things are recycled
whether leaf, feather, fur, or
the body of a saint.

Bad Moon Rising

*D*arlene glanced at the clock hanging over the register. It was four minutes after eleven, and the last customer was still perched on a stool at the luncheon counter eating a slice of pie. She finished sopping up the coffee, cider, and cola puddles from the tabletop of the booth nearest the door and pulled down the window shades hiding from view the jack-o-lantern, black cat, and owl cut-outs stuck on the storefront glass. Then, she walked in back of the counter, and slid her pencil and order pad onto the top shelf beside the bins containing extra sugar and artificial sweetener packets.

"Thanks," said the elderly customer from behind her. "That was real good."

"You're welcome, Mr. Suddi. See you tomorrow night."

"Right, tomorrow," the old man replied as he stood, buttoned up his sweater, then shuffled out the front door of *Raleigh's Delight*.

Darlene took off her apron, hung it up on a peg, and leaned over to check her make-up in the shiny chrome of the carbonated beverage dispenser. She liked to look at herself in the chrome—the faint crows' feet around her eyes were not visible. The mirrors in the ladies' room made her look thirty. But why shouldn't they? She was thirty-six.

Pushing open the swinging door to the kitchen, she hollered, "Stan. Everybody is out. I'm leaving."

She spotted the diner's owner, Stan Raleigh, scrubbing the griddle. Darlene liked the fact he did not just hire street kids to do all the dirty work, instead he pitched in and did some of the messy chores, too.

Stan looked up from the greasy slab of steel and asked, "Register closed down?"

"Yeah. Closed it before Mr. Suddamendala left. Tape is in the drawer."

"Tape," she muttered to herself. If the freaking grid had not gone down and screwed things up, computers would still be doing all the work.

"Thanks. Have a good night," called Stan from the sink as he plunged the scrub brush into the suds. "Don't forget to lock the door on the way out, especially tonight."

"No problem. But there shouldn't be any trouble, by now the trick-or-treaters are sleeping in their pods," Darlene responded as she reached under the luncheon counter and grabbed her pocketbook.

Darlene strolled out of *Raleigh's Delight* and slammed the front door. Slamming was not optional, since the door never locked if you closed it gentle-like. She jiggled the handle, just to double-check, and then, nodded at the cardboard skeleton jitterbugging on the other side of the door's glass pane. Finally, off duty, she tugged the rubber band out of her hair. She wore her hair tied back when waitressing, but when not at work, she loved the silky way it felt against her neck.

Darlene hurried down the sidewalk, smiling at the full moon that hung like a dinner plate on the wall of night. The 11:20 shuttle should be by any minute, and she was eager to get home. After popping a piece of chewing gum in her mouth, she looked at her watch: *11:21 pm.*

Tonight, she needed to be home on time—she was expecting company. Plus, she had forgotten to refill her ferret's bowl of dried kibbles. Not that the ferret was thin. Darlene suspected she had one of the few fat ferrets on the planet. Still, she worried that Claude might get into more trouble than usual if she was late coming home.

When she heard the squeal of brakes as the shuttle operator began to slow the mass-trans vehicle, she spit out her gum, wrapped it in a tissue, tossed it into a nearby waste bin, unwrapped a second piece, put the new gum in her mouth, and slid its wrapper into her uniform's pocket. Two pieces of gum would normally be excessive, but minty fresh breath was important tonight.

The shuttle pulled up to the curb, and Darlene got on and slipped into a seat about midway back. She crossed her legs, then pushed her uniform's skirt down towards her knees. It was not that she was modest, she just figured most people didn't want to see white-stockinged legs. For some reason, Stan thought white shoes and hose complimented the white cotton aprons his waitresses wore over their turquoise retro-look uniforms. And so, Darlene and the other waitresses at *Raleigh's Delight* wore the ugly things.

The shuttle had gone six blocks, when the driver stomped on the brakes to avoid smashing into a scooter which had suddenly changed lanes. Darlene grabbed the seat in front of her as the vehicle lurched. Across the aisle, a boy in his early twenties yelled a profanity. When he slipped a headset off of his ears, she heard drums, guitars, and singing. With the volume turned up so loudly, she suspected he would go deaf and have an artificial eardrum installed within a few years. Without warning, the music boy looked at Darlene and caught her staring.

She pressed her back against the seat and turned her face to the window. Outside the darkened glass, neon signs glowed red-orange, green, and purple as the shuttle zipped down the boulevard. Darlene knew if she had been walking by those storefronts instead of speeding along in a mass-trans vehicle, she would have heard the hum of the tubing. She supposed the hum had to do with the gas the manufacturers sealed in the glass tubes, but she wasn't sure of the science.

She knew the tubing was heated and formed. If you looked closely, you could see the glass near the connectors was singed and blackened. But few people noticed the dark glass—most only saw the colorful designs.

Shifting in her seat, she turned her attention to the reflections on the inside of the shuttle's tinted windows. She studied the images of the passengers, noting there were about twenty people on the shuttle, including some in costume. Two seats back, a young couple was kissing.

Her mouth curled as she remembered evenings spent with Jimmy Tyler beneath the trees in Uncle Cally's agro-orchard where the fruit hung dark and sweet. Jimmy, ha! She licked her lips. For a moment, she thought she felt him pressed up against her arm, and touched the plastic seat next to her thigh to make sure he hadn't gotten onto the vehicle without her noticing.

Darlene squinted, then looked at the window reflections again. The music boy was moving his head to the thumping beat coming from his earphones. Jimmy had done the same thing to songs by old-time rockers like Creedance Clearwater Revival. Last time she saw him, about an hour before he left for the hunting trip with his cousins, he was singing, *Bad Moon A-Rising*. She had told him to wear red, but he was never one for caution.

If only Jimmy had listened, she thought. *Then, things might have gone differently.*

The shuttle lurched again. A quick glance at the street markers told her the next stop was hers. She looked across the aisle. The music boy was still there, and he was studying her. Ignoring his stares, she stood and moved to the front of the shuttle. The vehicle hissed to a stop, and she got off and began to walk down Church Street.

It was little more than two blocks to her living quarters in an old warehouse which had been converted into six apartments. Usually, it was a pleasant stroll by three churches, a few Victorian-styled homes, and the Veterans Memorial Park. The VM Park occupied an odd-shaped grassy lot that had a few trees and shrubs, a fountain, some benches, and a memorial statue with the names of local war heroes engraved on bronze plaques attached to its base. Darlene liked to sit on one of its benches on her days off and read the paperback novels she picked up from Like New Second-Hand Books.

But tonight, the park's peacefulness was suddenly disrupted by raucous voices coming from behind her. Darlene stopped, then turned around. The music boy and two other men were following her.

"Hey," the music boy called. "Where you going in such a hurry?"

"Didn't you hear what my friend said?" asked one of the others.

Darlene bit her lip and walked as fast as she could. She saw the door to her apartment was only about fifty meters away.

"Slow down. We just want to ask you a question," said the music boy. He was about two meters behind her now.

Darlene looked for Jimmy, but saw no one on the street. She knew it wouldn't do any good to scream, so she broke into a run. The trio following her gave a whoop, and began to run, too. She had started up the steps to her door when one of the young men grabbed her shoulder.

Darlene reached into her purse, grasped the cold handle of one of Jimmy Tyler's old guns, and turned around to face her assailants. Security cameras had fallen victim to techno glitches associated with the grid failure. Thieves had made off with any remaining usable parts months ago, so whatever happened next, would remain a mystery.

The music boy grinned at her. Darlene noticed the gleam from her porch lantern was reflected by the blade of a knife he held in his left hand. Thankful that Jimmy had taught her how to shoot, Darlene pursed her lips and pulled the trigger.

The music boy fell like an apple to the ground. His two friends vanished, just like the mourners had after Jimmy's funeral. And Darlene was alone. She looked down at the body sprawled on the steps. The boy was obviously dead—dead and staring up at the stars.

As Darlene slid Jimmy's revolver back into her pocketbook, she recalled how Jimmy and she used to stare at the stars on August nights when the lawns were speckled with fireflies and owls, tree frogs, and cicada filled the air with song. She smiled. Those had been the best days of her life.

She heard a cough, or maybe it was the scuff of a shoe, and peered towards the corner of Church and Cemetery Streets. There was

Jimmy, still young and handsome, standing beneath the streetlight in the plaid shirt she had given him for his eighteenth birthday. He raised his hand. Darlene sighed and returned his greeting.

A siren in the distance caused her pulse to race as she stared down Church Street towards the main road. The emergency vehicle's whining reminded her of the siren on the ambulance that had taken Jimmy to the medical center the day he was shot—the day he had first left. As the shrill noise became fainter, her heart returned to its normal slow thumping, and she looked back at the corner. Jimmy was striding toward her.

Darlene wiped away the tears that threatened to spill down her cheeks. Tonight, the night when the dead could pass through the veil that separated them from the living, Jimmy would visit with Claude and her from the stroke of midnight until first light. Then, she'd accompany him back to the graveyard, kiss him one final time, and spend the next three-hundred-and-sixty-four days waiting for October 31st to roll around again.

Jimmy was strolling up the sidewalk to her door, and just before she felt his strong arms wrap around her, Darlene bent down, closed the music boy's eyes. Before going inside, Jimmy and she would carry the body to the graveyard and leave it leaning against a tombstone. It was an easy task, for she had chosen the location of her apartment with care—just across the street from the town's oldest cemetery.

Darlene hoped the dead boy had someone who loved him, someone to visit next Halloween. She shivered as Jimmy's lips met hers. But before she lowered her eyelids, Darlene glanced over his shoulder. In the golden glow of the Harvest Moon, she saw the music boy. His ghost had risen. It gaped at her with a confused look in its dark glassy eyes, and then, it turned and wandered down the trash-littered street.

Not Seen

The things I have not seen
when a chill neatly tucks
an errant strand of hair behind my ear
with tender fingers,

when a stray cloud-drop wets my lips
with a moist kiss,

when a draft strokes my back
with its icy palm,

when fog holds me close
in a clammy embrace,

when I awake mid-dream
and hear my name
whispered by the dark.

Beloved,
I studied your obituary, sleepwalked
through funeral parlor niceties,

listened to the service
for the burial of the dead,

witnessed dirt clods showering down
on your steel crate, but...

Oh, the things I have not seen.

A Salem Town Great-Granddaughter

*A*udra tilted the jack-o-lantern's lid back and blew out the candle, sending a cloud of scorched pumpkin smoke drifting through the room. Glancing behind her at Bern, asleep on the sofa beneath a crocheted afghan, she heard him cough, then mumble something unintelligible.

"Talking to the fairies, I guess," she said to the orange and white cat curled on the hearth.

The cat stood, stretched from toes to tail, yawned, then sat next to the fire-poker and ash shovel, waiting for Audra to put the boy and fire to bed for the night. As if to confirm the lateness of the hour, an owl whoo-whooed from a tree branch near the house.

"Okay, little man. Let's head to your real bed," she whispered. She rousted Bern and guided him, still wrapped in the afghan, to the small bedroom they shared.

With a sure and gentle hand, more fitting a mother than an older sister, Audra pulled down the top sheet and blankets, lifted him onto his cot, removed his shoes and socks, then covered him. Her brother had begged to stay up and answer the door when the trick-or-treaters came knocking, but at six years old, he had barely made it to eight o'clock. And thank goodness he was six. It made it easier for Audra to keep a job.

Leaving the door slightly ajar so the light from the fire and an old brass floor lamp painted a bright stripe across the bedroom floor, Audra returned to the main room of the tiny house they shared. A glance at the kitchen area confirmed she had picked up after dinner and placed two cereal bowls, two spoons, and two glasses on the counter for tomorrow morning's breakfast. And Bern's book bag was leaning against the wall by the door, packed and ready for school.

"I haven't forgotten you," she assured the cat as she scooped some dried cat chow into a chipped soup bowl and set it near the fireplace.

"Nor you," she said to the blaze as she placed a saucer with a pinch of salt and a bit of bread on the hearth and added fresh water to a glass baking dish located beside the cat food bowl.

Foolish superstition was what her grandmother called this nightly ritual. But Audra, like her mother before her, believed in magic. As the great-granddaughter several times over of Ann Pudeator, a woman hung hundreds of years ago on Salem Town's Gallows Hill for being a witch, Audra still carried the genetic mutation for magic. And she still believed in the possible—no matter how improbable.

Perhaps Gabeta was nothing more than a Lithuanian mythological deity, or perhaps she *was* the protector of home and family. Maybe leaving the salt and bread was wasteful nonsense, but in the morning, the birds would appreciate the uneaten bread. Besides, whether Gabeta chose to bathe in the backing dish water or not, the cat might want a drink.

As if she heard her thoughts, the cat strolled over to Audra and rubbed against her lower leg.

"What a good kitty. What a good kitty," she repeated affectionately as she scratched Ember's neck just below her left ear.

Seeming to demand even more attention, the cat pushed against her fingers. She obliged Ember, soothed by the softness of the animal's fur and the sound of her purring. Life was hard, and these quiet moments with the cat were a small pleasure after working

Monday through Friday as a cashier at the local food market, taking care of her brother, and helping out her cantankerous grandmother.

But she really should not complain about her father's mother. The New England saltbox house where Bern and she lived had been given to their mother by Grandmom and passed down to Audra upon Mom's death. At nineteen, it was just so exhausting to spend day after day as a substitute mom, dutiful granddaughter, and eight-to-four check out clerk.

After giving Ember a final pat, Audra stood and began to cover the coals in the fireplace with ashes so the fire would not wander. She had only scooped up one shovel full when a knocking came at the door.

Late trick-or-treaters, she thought as she set down the ash shovel and picked up a bowl of individually wrapped licorice sticks. When she opened the door ready to comment on the costumes of the little ghosts and ghoulies sure to be standing on her porch before giving them some candy, Ember began to yowl. Before she could *ssh* the cat or speak to the trick-or-treaters, three men shoved their way into the house.

Men was a term she was applying loosely. The creatures who stood before her, while human-like were definitely not human.

"How about sweets for your visitors?" growled one of the beings.

"Not much of a hostess," commented a second creature as he wrestled the bowl of candy from Audra's hands.

The third being scooted behind her quicker than a hornet, and slammed the door shut.

All Audra could think about was Bern. She had to keep her brother safe. She'd promised their mother she would protect him, and non-human or human thugs alike were not going to harm him as long as she was alive.

"Leave," she ordered and pointed at the door with a quavering finger.

"Don't think so," said one of the non-human men as he sat on the sofa. His colleagues joined him, each resting most comfortably on a cushion and tearing into the licorice like they hadn't eaten in a year.

Though repelled by the chomping and slurping, Audra could not help but stare as the three red capped, bulgy-eyed, stringy haired intruders gorged themselves on the licorice without removing the plastic wrappers.

Hoping the pointy eared trio wouldn't notice, Audra retrieved her cell phone from the kitchen counter to call the police.

"Not so fast," snapped one of the creatures as he gestured with his forefinger. The phone shot from her hand and flew across the room. A string of drool hung from the corner of his wide mouth.

"Not that police officers would do you any good," snickered another of the non-humans. "Don't think they have a protocol for goblins."

His comment set off a round of snorts and guffaws from the others.

Goblins, Audra thought. Well, at least she knew with whom she was dealing. But what to do for protection? If only Mom were here, she would have known what to do about goblins. Audra's magical skills were limited. Actually, *undeveloped* would be the better word, and her family's grimoire was hidden away in the cupboard in Bern's room.

Suddenly, she was aware of the silence. The goblins had finished the licorice and now looked at her with narrowed eyes.

"We need meat," said the tallest of the goblins.

"Fresh meat," added the heaviest goblin.

"Raw meat," said the goblin with especially long, sharp teeth.

"I am not sure what I have in the freezer..." Audra began.

"No need for a freezer," interrupted the heaviest goblin as he cracked his knuckles, then patted his belly. "You'll do."

"And I hear breathing in the next room," added the toothy goblin as he licked his upper lip. Which was the only lip he could lick, since his lower jaw jutted out and his teeth, four times as long as any bulldog's teeth, nearly reached his nostrils.

"No!" Audra stepped in front of the bedroom door and closed it.

"No," repeated the goblins as they laughed and withdrew three jagged butcher knives from their belts. "No?"

Before they could lunge at Audra, Ember began to growl. Not a get-out-of-my-way-stupid-dog growl, but a deeper, throatier growl that seemed to burst from the orange and white cat like an explosion. Her golden eyes locked on Audra's eyes, then she patted the hearth beside the bread and salt dish with her paw.

Bread and salt, thought Audra. *Bread and salt and bells might protect against goblins.* While the foul trio turned their attention and knives towards Ember, Audra backed into the kitchen, grabbed a salt shaker, a loaf of bread, and an old school bell. For years, the bell had perched on her mother's desk at the local high school where she had taught American history. With Mom's passing, its only purpose had been to remind Bern and Audra of her. Now, it might just save their skins from goblin blades.

"Mayhaps, we'll have cat for an appetizer," chortled the heaviest goblin as he closed in on Ember.

Audra sprinkled salt in front of the bedroom door.

"Cats are a little chewy, but tasty," said the long-toothed goblin as he spit into the fire.

In response to the spit, the flamelets roared into a blaze barely contained by the firebox. The flickering light illuminated the goblins' cruel faces, spike-like teeth, and sinewy arms.

Audra shredded a few pieces of bread and scattered the crumbs over the salt.

Ember growled again, then morphed into a cat made of fire. Slack jawed and glassy-eyed, the goblins seemed mesmerized by the flaming cat before them.

Audra gripped the school bell's handle tightly and began to ring the bell like there was no tomorrow.

The goblins were too spellbound to acknowledge Audra and the bell, instead they crouched, blades in hand, and crept towards the fire-cat.

With a sound like storm winds tearing through a Massachusetts sea town, the cat grew into a woman of terrible, flaming beauty. The fire-woman's eyes burned like two coals in her reddish gold face as she walked from the hearth and wrapped her blazing arms around the goblins in a searing embrace. In the time it took Audra to gasp, the trio of would-be murderers were ash.

Gabeta, for that was whom Audra knew she must be, returned to her hearth, shrunk to a fire-cat, then changed back into the orange and white feline who had lived in the house for as long as Audra could remember. Too long, in fact, for a normal cat.

"Audra! It's dark in here. I'm having bad dreams," cried Bern from the bedroom.

"Sorry. I'll open the door a bit," she answered in a trembling voice.

"You sound funny, Audra. Is something wrong?"

"No," she said to her little brother as she opened the door just a crack and gazed over at the orange and white feline grooming herself as she sprawled on the hearth. "Nothing Ember and I can't handle."

And after she had locked the front door, Audra swept up the bread, salt, and goblin soot. Then, she mixed them in with the ashes in the fireplace as she covered the coals to keep Gabeta from wandering.

"Thank you," she whispered to Ember and the fire. "I promise, I will read the grimoire and find someone to teach me about the Craft."

An empty licorice wrapper crinkled underfoot, the coals shifted, and the cat winked in response. And in the distance, Audra swore she heard Ann Pudeator, her great-grandmother many times over, whisper her blessing.

Harvest Mouse

I watch a mouse
lured by wheat berries and muffin crumbs
venture out
from dark, hidden burrow
beneath the japonica bush.

Gray velvet gatherer
of spillage from the bird-feeder,
ignored by sparrows,
she darts from hole to red-bud tree
in risky dusk.

Footprints like stitches
mark the white tablecloth of snow
spread under boughs bent
by starlings eager to swallow
a mouse's meal.

But I am not a rodent goddess
who blesses and protects careless mice.
Instead, I open wide my door,
loose
the hungry cat.

Gifts in the Dark

It was almost time to walk to the graves. The sun had vanished behind the Nodin Sea, the streetlamps were lit throughout the city of Halona, and the pair of owls that haunted Old Kurak's Medicines & Cure-Alls were calling for the dead.

"The dead," sighed Mari. This year, in addition to her parents, grandparents, great-grandparents, and other ancestors, she needed to remember Old Kurak, her Beloved, and his granddaughter, Little Nina.

Mari heard the clink of jar hitting jar as her sister loaded the food into the two picnic baskets they would carry to the graveyard. She quickly finished the last scarlet feather stitches on the tablecloth she was embroidering, tied a knot, and bit the unused tail of embroidery floss off close to the fabric with her teeth.

"Ready, Jacy," she said to the white cat watching her sew.

The cat chirped in response. He hopped down from his perch on the stone bench beside her and strolled to the doorway. Jacy paused, turned his mismatched eyes in her direction, and chirped again.

"I know, you miss her." Mari reached down, scratched the cat behind his left ear. "So do I." She stood, folded the tablecloth, and carried it into the kitchen.

She admired the two picnic baskets waiting by the door. They were painted with pink, teal, and violet birds and black and white skulls. In addition, they were festooned with bright ribbons and tiny bells. She smiled, then tucked the completed tablecloth into the side of the nearest basket. Jacy padded behind her chattering in cat-speak.

"He knows *Noche de los Muertos* is when we will remember his mistress," commented Mari's sister, Grace, as she slipped a beautifully carved comb embellished with ovals of polished turquoise into her gray hair.

"And dear Old Kurak." Mari bit her lip, brushed her deeply wrinkled cheek with the back of her hand. She was glad Grace did not respond right away. It gave her a moment to compose herself as they both slipped on woolen sweaters embroidered with geometric patterns, butterflies, and crows.

She glanced back at the kitchen table. The pale blue candles burning brightly in her grandmother's candelabra illuminated several platters heaped high with steaming vegetables, fresh fruit, and corn bread. Her great-grandmother's hand-thrown pottery bowl, nearly overflowing with red beans and rice, had been placed at the head of the table. A pitcher of tea and nine glasses sat beside it, and a stack of plates and eating utensils had been placed at the opposite end of the table. Should the dead decide to stop for dinner, they would be well-fed.

"Mari, it's time."

She nodded at her sister, and using a splinter of wood, lit the pair of white tapers nestled in carved wooden candlesticks on either side of the front door.

"For Grace, First-born," she said, and handed one of the carved candlesticks to Grace.

"For Mariposa, Second-born," her sister said as she picked up the remaining candlestick and handed it to Mari.

"We leave our home to bring you warmth," chanted Mari as she swung open the door.

"We carry candles into the darkness to bring you light," her older sister added in a sing-song voice.

The street was filled with men, women, and children. Some were traveling to the cemeteries with offerings. Some were walking to the beach to remember those who were missing at sea. Some were hurrying to parties and parades. Some were headed to the vendors to purchase skull masks, skeleton dolls and puppets, paper flowers, bundles of herbs, candles, fruit juice, and sweets. There was more commotion on *Noche de los Muertos* than on the busiest market day.

"Why wouldn't you accept his offer of marriage?" asked Grace as the two women picked up the baskets with their left hands while still holding the candles with their right, and stepped into the crowded street. "He asked you again and again."

"I wanted to wait until Little Nina was grown."

Mari did her best to ignore her tears. In order to wipe them away, she would have to set down the basket. Instead, she made a kiss-kiss sound at Jacy, who mewed in response, and then, walked beside her right ankle. The cat walked close, but not too close. He had been used to the long strides and dancing steps of a fifteen-year-old, but with Nina gone, he'd adjusted to the smaller strides and slower pace of a woman in her sixties.

"Nina would have been fine," observed Grace as they were jostled by the parade of celebrants heading up Nokomis Way towards the burial hill. "I think she would have welcomed a grandmother."

Mari did not answer her sister right away. She needed to pay attention to where she stepped, and she knew Grace should be careful, too. The cobblestones beneath their feet were littered with odd bits of food that had spilled from picnic baskets, flower petals, and scraps of colored paper. Dozens of dogs, some with ribbons tied around their necks, scampered here and there gulping down the dropped food. A gang of laughing boys with faces painted like skulls ran by them carrying skeleton puppets.

"With her parents gone, I didn't want Nina to think I was taking away her grandfather's love," explained Mari as the sisters neared the food vendors who had set up tables and carts at the entrance to Halona First Settlers Graveyard.

"Nina would not have minded. I think she'd have been happy to have you live with them. She was over Paco's house to visit with you often enough with that cat..."

"Mmm, look at the coffin bread," said Mari. She knew the delicacies heaped on the makeshift booths, tables, and vendors' carts by the local bakeries and confectioners' shops should distract Grace. Her sister was famous in their family for having a terrible sweet tooth and little willpower.

"Ah, *pan de muerto*. Do you think we should pick up a loaf or two before we visit the graves?" Grace ran the tip of her tongue across her bottom lip. "Or perhaps a few skull cakes or candied bones?"

Mari laughed and shook her head. After living together for decades, she could read her sister like pebbles tossed on a foretelling mat.

"I think we should wait until we finish at the graveyard."

Grace sighed. "I guess you are right. We will be carrying less when we walk down the road toward the sea."

Mari nodded in response. She did not want to think about the final part of tonight's ritual—did not want to think about standing on the beach sending the soul candles out to meet the Dark Lady.

They paused at the graveyard's gate, lifted high their candlesticks. The throng of celebrants around them did the same as they entered the graveyard. They joined the people of Halona as they sang the traditional Summoning Song:

Dear ones, beloved ones, we are now here
with honey jars, bread loaves, sea salt, and beer.
Dear ones, cherished ones, you are not alone —
bright blossoms and sweet herbs welcome you home.
Candles are borne to your dwelling places
as we pray to again see your faces.
Dear ones, treasured ones come to us tonight —
return to your children, return to light.

Mari and her sister sang the Summoning again and again. As they climbed to the highest reaches of the graveyard where their family's plots awaited tending, the singing of the other celebrants grew softer.

"Finally," exclaimed Grace as she set her basket down on a tidy grave. "It does not seem to be an honor to be one of the first families to settle in Halona when you have to drag a heavy basket up to the top of the burial grounds."

Mari tilted her head. A few gray hairs escaped their braids and fell around her face. "There is no use in complaining. Let's begin decorating the graves, and I'll tell the story of the Great Migration."

Her sister grunted her agreement and began to empty her basket.

"In the Olden Times, on Terra, the First Mother, there were many tribes and many nations. But humankind mistreated the First Mother, and she became sick. There was no cure for her illness, and she grew weaker and weaker, until she no longer had the strength to take care of the men and women who were her children."

Mari paused while she spread the embroidered tablecloth she had finished today on their parent's grave and traced a sacred symbol in the air with her forefinger.

"Sweets from the little messengers of the gods," repeated Grace as she dribbled honey on each of the graves of their loved ones.

"Even the Mother sheds tears for the dead," chanted Mari. She followed behind her sister sprinkling salt on each grave. Then, she resumed telling the ancestors' tale: "It was decided that a Great Migration would be embarked upon. All the tribes of Our People combined their languages, their power, their wealth—so when the Seed Ships were cast upon the Ocean of Stars, Our People had a place on each ship."

She set the salt jar back in the basket, picked up a loaf of fresh baked bread, and began to tear it into small pieces. The white cat at her feet stared up at her with his one green eye and one yellow eye. He seemed to be awaiting the rest of the story.

She spoke again. "The Seed Ships sailed for almost forever in the Ocean of Stars and Our People and all the other tribes of humankind slept the sleep of the dead. When they had just about given up hope, the Seed Ships reached the Shores of Forever. There, each ship found its island. Our Seed Ship found Earth Settlement Five—a new and unspoiled Mother. This new Mother, known to Our People as Anna Tuwa, welcomed her adopted children as if they were her own."

"And soon they were her own," added Grace. She poured beer on each grave and said in a sing-song voice, "Quench your thirst, Old Ones."

"Yes," agreed Mari. She stood, walked from grave to grave tossing breadcrumbs. "A bit of bread, a taste of life. Assuage your hunger, Old Ones," she sang in a melodious alto voice. Jacy followed her purring loudly.

After she had finished throwing crumbs upon the graves, Mari continued the ancestors' story. "But Our People did not come alone. We brought many animals with us, stored in glass bottles. When Seed Ship Five reached Anna Tuwa, the voyagers planted the animal seeds and grew the cattle, sheep, horses, chickens, dogs, and..." She smiled at Jacy, then continued, "the cats of the First Mother."

The sisters knelt at the foot of their oldest relatives' graves, placed a votive on each plot, and sprinkled marigold petals around the candle. It made sense to Mari that the pungent smelling petals of the *flowers of the dead* were bright sun colors. Wasn't daylight something the dead would miss?

As she lit the candles, Mari again spoke. "We also brought seeds for the totem animals of Our People. We brought the Wolf to remind us to persevere, we brought the Squirrel to make us laugh, we brought the wise Whale, the gentle Deer, the powerful Bear..." She stopped for a moment, thought of Old Kurak whose totem had been the bear.

"Go on," urged her sister as they moved to the next set of graves.

"And Turtle, who reminds us of creation and eternal life. And so, Our People settled with the other nations of humankind on our new home where we honor our new mother, Anna Tuwa, but we also honor our ancient traditions."

In silence, they decorated each remaining family grave with marigolds and votives. Finally, they placed a bundle of sage, rosemary, and other sacred herbs beside each candle. Then, both women knelt, lifted their arms to the moon, and chanted the Summoning Song again.

"Dear ones, beloved ones..."

When they finished the chant, the sisters stood and prepared to depart. Jacy wound around Mari's ankles mewing. She suspected he wanted her to pick him up. But with basket in her left hand and candle in her right, she still had her hands too full to carry a cat.

Though there was no breeze to speak of, suddenly, her candle's flame flickered and almost went out. Grace elbowed her, pointed with a shaky hand at two shadows passing back and forth across their parents' graves.

"They have come back to us," her sister whispered. "Perhaps it is our time to go with them when they return to the Land of the Dead at dawn."

"Look." Mari nodded in the direction of the metal fence that surrounded their family's plot on three sides. The pair of owls who perched over Nina's old bedroom every night had swooped down and alighted on the fence. One of the birds clutched a dead snake in its talons. The owls tilted their heads, the one with the snake dropped its scaly body onto a grave. Then, the pair lifted up with a silent flap of wings and flew into the night sky.

"What do you think it means?" There was no mistaking the fearful quaver of Grace's voice.

Mari shrugged her shoulders. "The Snake is a symbol of transformation, of change, of rebirth. Perhaps they were sent to us by the Old Ones to comfort us."

"I do not feel very comforted," muttered her sister as they headed down the hill to the cemetery's entrance.

By the time they exited Halona First Settlers Graveyard, Grace seemed to have forgotten the owls. Instead, she was focused on buying skull cakes, candy bones, and coffin breads. But Mari could not erase the look in the eyes of the night birds from her mind. The owls had seemed to be trying to tell her something. But what?

"Are you sure you don't want a bite?" asked her sister as she licked sugar granules from her fingers. "I believe these skull cakes are the sweetest ones I have ever tasted."

"No. We need to head to the beach before it gets any later."

"I suppose you are right." Her sister gave the skull cakes another longing look, and then joined Mari and Jacy as they began the journey to the edge of the Nodin Sea.

Young women dressed in vivid blouses and ruffled skirts scurried by them. Groups of young men tooting on horns, strumming guitars, and banging on small drums marched up and down the roadway. Children ran by trying to get black kites edged with golden stars to lift up into the night sky. Clusters of old women gossiped on the street corners. Mari and Grace waved to many of them.

"*The Night of the Dead* is one of my favorite holidays."

Mari glanced at her sister. Her eyes sparkled, her forehead glistened with beads of perspiration, and there were cake crumbs clinging to her top lip. *Noche de los Muertos* did seem to agree with her.

"I smell the sea," said Grace as she took several deep breaths.

Mari's throat tightened. Her sister was right. They were almost at the end of Nokomis Way where the cobblestones gave way to pebbles and the pebbles merged with the sand. Before them she saw the hissing froth of the waves racing across the beach and the towering flames of the Lighting Fire.

There were dozens of people milling about the water's edge. Some held torches, others candlesticks. Most had already sent their soul candles out to the Dark Lady. A few were still placing paper boats on the sand, setting a small lit candle in the boat, and letting the waves carry the fragile vessels out into the great darkness of the night sea.

The chant said on the shore was less hopeful than the Summoning Song. The souls of those lost in the waters of the Nodin or the waters of some distant ocean that most of the people of Halona had never heard of were given into the care of the Dark Lady. Tonight, Mari and her sister would send two boats out into the Nodin—one for Old Kurak and one for Nina.

Mari sighed, set her basket on the sand. When Grace's son-in-law, Paco, and the other nestgatherers had returned from the ill-fated nestgathering expedition this spring, the news quickly spread that Old Kurak and Little Nina had died in the collapse of an island cave. Their bodies would never be recovered, never carried with honor to the graveyard of their ancestors. And so, this sacred night, Mari and her sister would remember two people who were dear to them and give their souls over to the Dark Lady.

Mari and Grace each unpacked a paper boat from their baskets. They each lit a tiny candle and set it in the vessels.

"There, there," said Mari to the cat who cried at her feet.

Jacy continued to wail. He batted at one of the paper boats and tried to upset its candle.

"Hush, little cat," crooned Mari. She picked up Jacy, cradled him in her arms as the waves drew closer to the paper boats.

Grace touched her arm. "It is time."

Mari closed her eyes for a moment, recalled Old Kurak's loving face and gentle touch. Then, she thought of Nina's ready smile and quick mind. She opened her eyes, began the Chant of the Lost:

Dear ones, beloved ones, where are your bones?
Beneath the cold waves? Across the deep sea?
Dear ones, cherished ones, you are far from home
and so we give you to the Dark Lady.
She will gather your souls and dry your tears.
She will sing you to sleep and hold you near.
Dear ones, treasured ones, you are gone forever
and your sweet faces we will see again never.

"Old Kurak. Little Nina," said Grace.

"Beloved Kurak. Dearest Nina," whispered Mari.

Together, they repeated the Chant of the Lost as the waves carried their little candle-lit boats out into the darkness. Jacy meowed loudly, squirmed in Mari's arms. She set him upon the sand where he paced back and forth yowling.

Grace put her arm around Mari's waist. "It will get easier as time passes. We still have each other, Paco's family, our sewing, and the cat."

"But is it enough?" Mari could barely make out the light from one of the little boats, but the other seemed to be returning to shore.

As the paper boat drew closer to the beach, a murmur passed through the crowd. Such a thing was unheard of. For the Dark Lady to send back a soul candle meant that the person remembered was not dead. There was a flash of lightning and a strange phosphorescence shimmered on the surface of the sea. A shining woman rose from the midst of the phosphorescence. She appeared to point at the sisters.

Mari squinted. She could make out two large birds perched on the shining woman's shoulders.

Several village women screamed as the birds took off, soared into the air, and skimmed across the waves towards shore. One of the birds, which Mari could now identify as owls, plucked the soul candle from the boat. It screeched, then flew to Mari, Grace, and Jacy.

The stunned crowd backed away from the sisters and the white cat as the two owls landed, placed the still-burning soul candle in front of Mari. The owl who had not transported the candle dropped a necklace of polished obsidian chips in front of Jacy.

"That necklace belonged to Nina," gasped Grace.

"Belongs," corrected Mari as the owls gazed up at her with their magical eyes. "That necklace belongs to Nina."

The crowd began to chant. At first their chanting was barely audible, but it steadily grew until the night seemed to be filled with the shouts of the living calling home Nina from the Land of the Dead. The owls circled three times above the throng of *Noche de los Muertos* celebrants before returning to their shimmering mistress.

And as the moon-pale cat picked up the necklace with his pearly teeth, the Dark Lady, Queen of the Dead and Comforter of the Dying, sank into the cold, rippling waters of the sea.

Ocean Lure

Strolling on an empty beach,
I saw a mermaid reclining on a jetty.

Swathed in moonlace,
she combed the flossy strands
that swirled around her like kelp.

Foam caught on sequined thighs
as she flicked her tail
and sang a ballad
about ships and sailors and forever.

When the shoreward wind rattled a trash can,
she turned aqua eyes to study me.

My throat constricted.

The gulls mimicked her laughter
as she slipped beneath gyrating water.

Chilled,
I hurried back to the hotel
to check on my sons.

The Burryman

With only a blanket between him and the horse's backbone, Fen knew there was no comfortable way to ride the mare through town. Still, it must be done. The local Fishermen's Guild had chosen him to raise the herring. But it was not just the honor of being Burryman that kept him seated on Sallie's back, the reward for participating in this ceremonial parade would bring his great uncle and him enough wealth to last a lifetime. And it had been more than ten lifetimes since the ocean had demanded a Burryman.

Burryman! Fen carefully shook his head. Dozens of dead herrings dangling from the brim of his hat swung back and forth. Like most of the people of the village, until recently he had not heard of a Burryman before. But after the sixth month of poor fishing, Guildmaster Galen had searched the vault in the Fishermen's Guild House and located the tattered sheepskins that explained the ancient ritual.

Fen's mount flicked her ears and stamped her right front hoof. As she swished her tail, he watched the skin on her shoulder twitch. Unable to find much man-skin exposed, the flies buzzing around his hat were alighting on the horse and biting her.

"We have almost got everything in order," said his best friend, Oswin, as he patted Fen's boot.

"Great!" He tried to sound enthusiastic. "Hopefully, the flies will leave Sallie alone once we start moving."

Oswin nodded, and adjusted his grip on the wooden wheelbarrow he would be pushing the length of the parade route.

Fen sighed. The owls had only minutes before returned to their roosts. The sun had barely crested the hilltops and perspiration already trickled down his neck. Though necessary to prevent injury, the long sleeved undershirt and thick flannel outer-shirt he wore beneath a layer of burdock burrs made him overdressed on this muggy summer morning. Added to that, burr-covered chaps had been lashed onto his legs and on his hands he wore knitted gloves. Luckily, burrs had only been embedded in the top of the gloves, which allowed Fen to hold the reins of the mare's bridle.

"Piper is ready." Oswin grinned up at him. "Got any requests?"

"Yes. Something mellow, so Sallie doesn't trot." Fen patted the white mare's neck. He had replied in jest, but riding a horse wasn't one of his skills. If Sallie clopped along at any pace quicker than a walk, Fen had no doubt without the benefit of a saddle, he would tumble off his mount in front of the whole village. Being selected Burryman had brought him more attention than he was comfortable with, and he did not want to add to his notoriety.

"Nothing too fast," shouted Oswin to the piper who waved a hand in response.

As the piper began inflating the pipes, the groans and wails emitted by the instrument caused the ceremonial nanny goat to bleat and dance about. The crowd of fishermen and townsfolk that had gathered behind the piper, Fen on Sallie, Oswin ready to push the barrow, and Guildmaster Galen holding the goat's lead cheered and laughed.

"And so it begins," yelled Oswin as the piper, leading the Burryman Parade and playing a traditional tune, began the hike from the village outskirts to the sea.

The first place they stopped was Stone-above-Sea Manor. The occupants, from lord to lowliest servant, emptied out of the manor house. They clapped and sang along with the ballad the piper was playing, then tossed money into the wheelbarrow. The lord made a great show of placing a handsome sum of coins into the wooden pushcart, but Fen knew this was a fraction of what he had paid to remove his sons' and nephews' names from the Burryman lottery.

Though the chance of an ocean god showing up at the end of the parade to claim the Burryman were slim to none, nevertheless any family wealthy enough to be able to pay the removal fee had done so. Three days ago, when the lottery was held, the Guildmaster's fish basket had only contained twenty-seven names. After ringing the town's summoning bell three times, Galen had plucked an oyster shell from the basket.

"The ocean keeps his fish from our nets," the Guildmaster had said while holding the chosen shell to his chest. "The clam beds are near barren," he had continued with a wide sweep of his empty hand. "And these brave lads have offered themselves as payment to the ocean, should he decide to claim them, so the town and its people can survive."

A cheer had risen up from the crowd gathered in the village square.

Then, Guildmaster Galen had glanced at the name on the oyster shell and announced, "Fen. Fen Dimond will be the Burryman."

Again, the crowd cheered. Fen was picked up by Oswin and several other friends, hoisted onto their shoulders, and carried around the square. Chants of "Fen, Fen, Fen" and "Burryman, Burryman, Burryman" rang out. But what Fen recalled most, was the look of horror on his great-uncle's face. Though well-educated, Uncle Isham was a superstitious man who still believed in merrows, selkies, and worse. Uncle Isham had made a warding sign in the air and spit on the cobblestones at his feet.

Y*ou and your uncle will be rich," hollered up Oswin as he set* down the wheelbarrow.

"We had better be." Fen pointed at his herring decorated headdress. "Just for putting up with this stinking hat, I deserve a year's wages."

Oswin laughed. "I think your reward will be more like a lifetime's worth," he answered as another group of townspeople tossed coins into the barrow and joined the throng parading to the shore.

As the crowd grew, the piper changed from marches to hornpipes and strathspeys. The livelier tunes with sea themed words and faster tempos caused the white mare to lift her head and walk more quickly. Fen grabbed onto Sallie's mane with his left hand while continuing to hold her reins with his right.

Several people with drums and flutes had joined the Burryman's Parade. The trilling of the flutes excited the goat. She high-stepped, bleated, swung her head, and kicked her back feet out. And the rhythmic thumping of the bodhrans seemed to control the clopping of Sallie's hooves.

At the start of the procession, Fen glimpsed only slivers of distant water; now, he could see the wide ocean between the houses. Looking bluer and more calm than usual, the water promised coolness, fresh air, and the end to the Burryman Parade. Three things he needed. A sultry noontime, dead fish, flies, the pounding of drums, and drone of bagpipes were causing his head to throb.

Once Fen removed his costume, he doubted he would linger for very long in the village square. Granted there would be dancing, tasty victuals, and ale to savor. And with his newly awarded wealth, he'd be able to approach the unmarried daughters of the town fathers. Even though he had turned eighteen in early spring, his limited salary had made it near impossible to court an eligible maid.

Fen glanced at the dozens of available young women walking nearby. Their faces were flushed. Some wore caps, some were bareheaded so waves of hair tumbled down their backs. They all were singing, clapping their hands, and laughing. One girl with a sprinkling of freckles across her nose and thick red hair caught him staring.

She smiled shyly.

Fen shifted his gaze. His face felt even hotter.

"Almost to the square," Oswin yelled. "You will be able to take that stinking hat off soon."

"Not soon enough," he responded.

Guildmaster Galen turned his head in Fen's direction and said in a voice louder than he thought the older man could manage, "The hat cannot be removed until after the ceremony." For emphasis, the goat Galen was leading looked at Sallie and Fen and bleated.

"I understand," Fen replied. With effort, he kept a serious expression on his face as Oswin bobbled his head and rolled his eyes at the Guildmaster's solemn admonishment.

Still holding the handles of the gift filled wheelbarrow, Oswin gestured with his head at a bespeckled man standing beneath a wooden sign with a carved owl and quill that read, "Dimond & Dimond." "There is your uncle."

And indeed, a frowning Uncle Isham was waiting for the Burryman's Parade in front of the small house crammed between the poulterer's shop and an apothecary on Commerce Street that Fen and he shared. The dour expression on his uncle's face was unusual. But Uncle Isham had heard horrible tales in his childhood about the ocean claiming a Burryman in the long-ago days of the first settlers, and fretted the worse would happen to his great-nephew.

Which seemed odd to Fen. Isham Dimond was a learned man. He could read, write, and calculate numbers—skills in limited supply in a seaside village. He had taught Fen those skills, and now they both helped with bookkeeping, tax calculations, and writing letters and official documents for a number of the town's small businesses and well-to-do individuals. "Dimond & Dimond" made enough profit to keep them fed, clothed, and under roof. But educated or not, Isham remained a true believer in archaic legends.

Uncle Isham stepped into the road as the Burryman Parade approached. The marchers gave way so Isham could walk at the side of his nephew.

"I will see this through with you, lad," called his uncle as he patted the horse's shoulder. "I would face down a kraken if need be to save you."

Fen smiled at the elderly man. "You worry overmuch, Uncle."

Isham pursed his lips, gripped his cane tighter, and patted the mare again. "I hope you are correct," he said, though the scowl on his face indicated he held little hope that the monsters of the deep were not going to show up and devour his nephew a few minutes from now.

As they reached the village square, Guildmaster Galen raised his hand and signaled it was time to raise the herring.

"We have offended the ocean. He refuses us his bounty. And so, we bring a scapegoat, white mare, and strong youth as offerings. Let us proceed to water's edge."

The crowd grew more solemn as Galen pointed to a finger of land jutting into the water and led the nanny goat towards that rocky spit. Fen on Sallie, Uncle Isham, and Oswin struggling to propel the overflowing barrow on sand followed. The crowd hung back, going only as far as the beginning of the beach.

A few yards onto the sand and pebbles of the seashore, Galen raised his hand again. "Oswin present the Burryman's family with the town's gifts."

Oswin set down the wheelbarrow, wiped his brow with the back of his arm, and stepped back. Isham Dimond leaned down and tapped one of the handles. "Is there one who would now assume this honor and claim these gifts?"

The townfolk were silent. No one volunteered.

Fen saw a look of defeat sweep across his great-uncle's face like a shadow.

"Then, it is done," Isham said as he pressed a hand to his chest.

Galen nodded. He stepped to the edge of the water. Fen and Sallie followed, then moved to stand alongside the Guildmaster.

"Burryman, dismount and await the decision of the sea," shouted Galen as he plucked a wicked looking knife from his sleeve.

Garbed in burrs and unused to riding horses, Fen did his best to get down from Sallie's back. Fortunately, the unsecured blanket beneath him made his slide off of the mare relatively easy and pain free. Still, Sallie rolled her eyes back and nickered at him. He supposed a burdock burr or two had poked her during his clumsy descent.

No sooner had his boots touched the sand then the water at his feet started to boil. Small silvery fish by the thousands appeared in the spume that flowed across the beach. The townsfolk gasped and ran forward. They scooped up the herring in their aprons and hats. Many of the men removed their shirts and filled them with the shimmering fishes.

"We offer a scapegoat to you. Forgive our offenses," called Guildmaster Galen as he untied the now wilted flower garland from the goat's neck and cast it into the surf.

Suddenly, dozens of pale goat heads broke the surface of the water. One of the seagoats paddled towards Galen and his charge. Fen could see the creature had two front legs that ended in thick webbed fins instead of feet and a large scaled tale instead of back legs. As the beast dragged itself from the ocean, its seaworthy appendages transformed into four hooved legs. Though its shape now appeared more normal, the seagoat was covered not by fur, but by glimmering whitish blue scales. And its tail, beard, and the tufts above its hooves were not long strands of hair, but fine tentacles that moved as if they had a will of their own.

The nanny, which had pranced and bleated though out the Burryman's Parade, stood still as stone as the sea creature studied it with limpid blue eyes. In his peripheral vision Fen caught the nervous movement of Galen's fingers on the knife handle. The seagoat nodded, backed away from the Guildsmaster and goat, and returned to the briny water. As soon as it was chest deep in the billows, the animal's hooves and back legs mutated back into their original form.

Again, the water at shore's edge filled with squirming fish. But this time, the fish were larger. Again the townspeople rushed forward and gathered the bounty.

Next, Galen shouted, "We offer a white mare to you. Forgive our offenses." He scooped up the beautifully woven horse blanket from where it lay on the beach and flung it into an out-going beachcomber.

As before, the mirror of the ocean was broken. This time, dozens of horse heads split the surface.

The villagers behind Fen muttered among themselves and took a step back.

Like the seagoat before him, a kelpie swam to the land's edge, and his finned front feet and tail changed into the four hooved legs of a land horse when he pulled himself from the brine. The kelpie, whose eyes were greener than the inland forests, was covered in pale lime scales that refracted light like the rarest gems. And there was no doubt this time that his mane, tail, and fetlocks were writhing tentacles.

Sallie froze. The kelpie, who stood about two hands taller than the mare, stretched his neck out and nuzzled the land horse. He snorted, gave first Galen, and then Fen, a long look. Seemingly satisfied the offering was made in good faith, the sea horse turned, trotted back into the water, and transmuted into his kelpie form.

The aqueous equine had barely swum back to deeper water to join his herd, when wavelets began to fling oysters, mussels, clams, and scallops onto the beach. A cheer went up from the townspeople. Giddy with thoughts of full bellies and possible pearls, they surged forward. Armloads of shell fish were seized and toted to each villager's pile of sea-plunder.

Without warning, a landward wind whipped the waves and spewed hunks of froth and seaweed on to the people. The skies darkened to a twilight grey. The frightened goat and mare yanked themselves from Galen's and Fen's grasps and fled.

"Remove your burrs and throw them into the ocean," the Guildmaster ordered.

Fen obeyed. First, he took off the gloves and flung them into the surf. Next, he unlashed the leggings and hurled them into the sea. Then, he grabbed his dead-herring-decorated hat and sent it sailing into a swell. Finally, he tore the Burryman shirt from his back and pitched it into the ocean.

When the burr-covered garments had vanished below the churning saltwater, Galen lifted his hands to the sky and shouted, "We offer a Burryman to you. Forgive our offenses."

From the sea's surface about a dozen yards from land rose a manlike being. There was no doubt in Fen's mind that this was an Old One—a godlike race that existed before the time of men.

The Old One, covered in purple and indigo scales from his calves to his forehead, was five times the height of a villager. A hard helmet of shells perched on his hair – hair that dangled from his head and merged with his mustache and waist-length beard in a wriggling mass of violet tentacles. Stiff, scalloped fins projected from his knees, lower arms, shoulders, and spine. In his clawed and webbed fingers, he clenched a trident that appeared to be made of metal. But it was his eyes that demanded attention. They were paler than pearls with an unnatural sheen that reminded Fen of a dead man.

As the Old One spoke, Fen realized that he alone remained standing. The villagers behind him and the Guildmaster beside him had fallen to their knees.

"You have called, and I have come bringing with me the fish that you seek," said the sea giant in a voice that sounded like waves crashing against pilings. "The goat and horse are fine offerings, but I require them not. The Burryman though, is needed."

Fen's legs felt like jelly as the Old One continued, "One of my daughters desires a human mate. The Burryman will suffice."

When the sea giant stopped speaking, the water at his ankles bubbled and a woman-like sea creature sitting sideways on the back of a kelpie appeared. Unlike her father, the female was of human size. She had dark brown hair, turquoise eyes, and scaly orange and gold skin. The strangely beautiful being, who wore a headdress similar to her father's, was garbed in a gown made of viridian and ultramarine fish scales. She opened her lips as if to speak.

"Wait!" Uncle Isham jumped to his feet and hurried to Fen's side. "Let the lad live a normal life. Take me instead."

The Old One chuckled—a chuckle that sounded like thunder. "And why would my daughter settle for a wrinkled fool when she can have a young man?"

All eyes turned to Isham Dimond.

"It is alright, Uncle. I..."

"Hush." Uncle Isham squeezed his arm. Then, the town scribe, accountant, and writer of letters pulled back his shoulders, lifted his head, and stared at the sea giant. "Legend says you must change any man who agrees to live in the deep with your lovely daughter. Most likely, after the transformation, that man will be given long life. So what difference does it make how old they are in human years?"

Both the Old One and his daughter studied Fen's uncle. Then, they turned their alien eyes towards Fen.

"He is correct, Father," said the daughter of the ocean in a voice like rivulets washing over rocks.

"Why?" inquired the sea giant.

"A gale took my nephew's parents, grandfather, and their fishing boat when he was but a child. Weeks later, his grandmother sickened and died from bad shellfish. Fen has already paid a heavy tax to the sea."

"And you?" boomed the Old One.

"In human years, I am nearing the end of my life. My eyesight grows worse, so soon I will be unable to work. And," Uncle Isham paused, looked at Fen. "And I have known love, if only for a brief time, while this lad has yet to find it."

"Where is this love you speak of?" asked the sea giant's daughter in her liquid voice.

"Dead. Long dead." Isham Dimond lifted his hands, then let them drop to his sides. "She fell from a horse and broke her neck two days before we were to be married. I buried her on our wedding day."

The daughter of the sea lowered her eyelids slightly and tilted her head. "And did she have hair blacker than the darkest night?"

"Yes," whispered his uncle as the sea-woman's hair turned ebony.

"And did she have skin whiter than a gull's breast?"

"Yes," murmured Fen's uncle as the sea-woman's skin became smooth and faded to the color of the palest shell.

"And were her eyes the green-grey of the ocean on a cloudy day?"

Speechless, Isham Dimond nodded as the sea-giant's daughter took on not only new eye color, but her whole face metamorphosed into that of the young woman Fen saw every day in the miniature portrait his great-uncle kept by his bed.

"Leah!"

"Isham," replied the daughter of the ocean. "Come, let us spend eternity together."

Fen turned, gazed at his uncle's joyful face. It shone with an unnatural light. As he watched, Uncle Isham's wrinkles smoothed, his sunken chest and thin arms swelled with muscles, his gnarled fingers straightened, and his diminished height returned to its youthful six-foot three-inch stature. He saw gills similar to those on the Old One and his daughter open in his great uncle's neck.

The youth that was Isham Dimond removed his spectacles and handed them to Fen. "For your old age, nephew."

"Wait, are you sure you want..."

"Wheel the coins home. Celebrate in the square. Find your true love. And remember me to your children," said Isham as he hugged Fen.

"I will never see you again." Fen felt his throat constrict. His great-uncle had been the most important person in his life. The house, the office, the days would seem empty without Uncle Isham.

"Perhaps." His uncle smiled, took a step back, pressed the palm of his hand against Fen's chest. "But I will live here and," he pressed his palm against his own chest. "And you will live here."

The daughter of the ocean in her Leah form had slipped from her kelpie and now stood in knee deep water with her left hand outstretched. "We must depart," she urged as her black-as-the-darkest-night hair fluttered in the sea breeze and her whiter-than-a gull's-breast skin glistened with ocean spray.

"Fare thee well, nephew," said a young Isham as he took the sea-woman's hand and ran to thigh high water. His great-uncle looked back once, winked, and dove into an incoming wave.

The Old One raised his trident, pointed it at Fen. "Go back to your land-life, Burryman. And mourn not your uncle. He has been rewarded for his sacrifice, as you have been rewarded for yours."

Then, scanning the village folk who remained kneeling with faces upturned and eyes opened wide, he added, "Do not offend the ocean again. Next time, I might not be so eager to accept your apologies." Warning issued, the sea giant accompanied by his kelpies, seagoats, daughter, and Isham Dimond vanished beneath the waves.

Fen felt a hand on his shoulder. "Come along. Let's push this wheelbarrow back to your house, then join the celebration," said his best-friend, Oswin.

Guildmaster Galen nodded in agreement, then mused, "I wonder where that goat and horse have run off to?"

And as the three men followed the chattering townfolk who were lugging an abundance of fish towards the square, Fen noted a pretty girl with red hair and a scattering of freckles across her nose lagging behind her parents. She smiled, and shyly gazed at him with sparkling gray-green eyes.

Leaf and Fish

How clear it seems —
something we knew all along
but had forgotten
until river water washed
over shimmering fins and leaves.

How delightful
the patterns on patterns,
veins on scales, spots on striping
that flowed around the mossy boulders
balanced one atop another.

How poignant the fish dream
of rising into the blue lake of heaven
and nibbling stars
with mouth round as the full moon's
reflection.

How final the leaf dream
of diving into the cascade
and tumbling with stones
until there is nothing remaining
but fine sand.

How natural it seems:
fish is leaf, firmament is sea,
star is firefly, pebble is moon,
and we are brothers, sisters
of them all.

By the Sea

*O*n this night, as the moon bobbed in the hungry sea, no
chorus rose from the brine to call to the sailors to shed their
uniforms. No tenors chanted a seductive melody sweet enough to lure
the sternest crewman to his grave. On this night, the water gurgled,
the flood tide rose, and mermen heaved their muscled bodies out of
the waves. Beneath a star-strewn sky, they lifted their whiskered heads
above the backwash like the first amphibians, traded their melodic
voices for legs, and raced across the beach to the boardwalk to try their
luck at games of chance.

The carnival workers grinned at these first time marks,
recognizing them by the bits of seaweed caught in their hair. They
laughed at their cash boxes filled with pearls and tarnished coins.
The mermen strolled the midway and tried the darts, the ring
throws, the basketball hoops, the bingo wheels, the coin tosses,
and gun shoots. The mermen were never victorious. The games
were not rigged, just difficult enough to defeat the inexperienced,
and the merfolk had not yet discovered the tricks for winning.

The mermen's eyes reflected the gaudy lights of the carousel.
They pointed at the rides, then hobbled to the Ferris wheel. After
clamoring into the seats, they wrapped their finely webbed hands
around the steel safety bars. Dusana felt herself squeezed between two

of the mermen as they sailed above the sea in the Ferris wheel bucket. She saw the gulls patrolling the sand, the rock jetties, the distant boats, and the stars that seemed to spread in a continuous skein from the sky through the horizon line into the dark water.

One of the merfolk faced her and opened his mouth to speak.

D*usana.*" *The girl felt someone shaking her shoulders.* "Dusana, wake up." She opened her eyes. "Tomas will be furious. It is nearly nine, and you haven't eaten or gotten into your costume." Eva's hands fluttered in front of her like two frightened doves. The middle-aged woman sighed loudly as she pulled open a dresser drawer, withdrew a spangled bikini top and one-piece pull-on.

"It will only take me a few minutes to get dressed and grab something to eat." Dusana promised as she sat up, seized a plastic bristled brush from the nightstand, and began untangling her hair. She tied her brown locks back in a ponytail and crawled into her wheelchair to make the trip to the toilet. Eva often reminded Dusana that her ability to go to the bathroom normally was a miracle. Most babies born with sirenomelia were missing internal organs and did not live to see their first birthday. Dusana was seventeen.

When she returned to her bedroom, Dusana bent her knees, slid into her tail sleeve, and tugged the upper portion of her costume over her hips. She slipped off her nightshirt and put on the bathing suit top and a zipper jacket emblazoned with the words: Dusana— Mermaid of the Deep.

Before she wheeled herself out of her bedroom, Dusana paused, picked up a photograph from the bedside table. In the faded picture, a group of sideshow performers stared into the camera as they posed on either side of Eva and Dusana. But Eva was not looking at the camera; instead, she gazed at Dusana as she held the little mermaid baby in her lap.

"Breakfast." Eva's husky voice called from the kitchen.

Dusana put the photo back on the nightstand and grabbed a flowing blond wig from a hook by the doorway. Tomas forced her to wear the wig.

"Customers want their mermaids blond," he would say every time she tried to convince him that her fawn colored hair would look lovely highlighted by the undulating lights of her under-the-sea themed room in the sideshow tent. "The mermaid on the banner has yellow hair. You gotta have yellow hair, or it'd be false advertising," he would lecture.

More than once, Dusana had offered to dye her hair blond.

"The wig is thicker, longer, more golden than real hair," Tomas had said. "Besides, the people want to be fooled, so we fool them."

Sometimes, Eva would speak up for Dusana. Remind Tomas that the wig itched and was hot in the summer beach heat.

"Silence," her husband would order. "I am Tomas Chaloupek, the oldest twin of Chaloupek Brothers' Amazing Oddities. I decide who wears what."

And that would end the conversation. Eva would puff out her cheeks several times, glare at her husband, then head for the ticket booth. Tomas would nod, stride to the bally platform. And Dusana would wipe away the perspiration, secure her fake golden tresses, and wheel herself to her place in The Tent of Human Oddities.

As she entered the kitchen, Tomas barked, "You're late," at Dusana before resuming the daily morning quarrel with his brother Silny, the Tattooed Man.

In addition to being an astounding achievement in body art, Silny was a weightlifter. When he put on his part of the show, Silny flexed his oiled muscles, assumed a number of body-builder poses, and lifted a barbell. Dusana did not know how much the barbell weighed; she just knew that Tomas and Silny collected bet money from audience members who thought they could lift Silny's barbell. No spectators had been able yet to lift it.

"Do you see this stack of bills?" Tomas waved a wad of paper in Silny's face.

"What can I say—people don't go to sideshows no more." Silny slurped his coffee. "We're not the only ones feeling the pinch—even the rides don't get the crowds they used to."

"That's 'cause the rides are old fashion—no special effects." Tomas leaned back in his chair and massaged his temples with his fingers. "We need to find a way to get more customers to walk through the tent flaps. Maybe some special effects could help us."

"You should check around. Come up with somebody who does that sort of thing," said Silny as he stuffed the last of his eggs in his mouth. "Can't hurt."

"But it'll be another bill, and where do you think I'll get the money for…"

Dusana tuned out Tomas and Silny, rolled her wheelchair to the kitchen table. Eva placed a mug of coffee and a plate of eggs in front of her. "Thank you," she whispered.

Eva smiled, returned to cleaning up the breakfast mess. The brothers left the house a few minutes later, still arguing. Dusana finished eating, took her dirty dishes over to the sink. "Have you ever heard of the surgery that separates fused legs?"

Eva's sallow complexion paled. "No, and never speak of this to Tomas. Besides, such a thing would be too expensive for carnival workers."

"But what if it didn't cost us anything?" Dusana closed her eyes for a second, thought about the merchandise displayed in the clothing store windows. She loved to peer through the glass at the newest fashions as she traveled up and down the boardwalk in the evenings. "Then I could wear shorts and blue jeans and high heels."

"Dusana, are you not fed? Clothed? Did I not see to it you got schooling?"

"Yes, but…" Dusana knew Tomas and Eva had found her abandoned in one of their tents. They had made the necessary arrangements with the government people. Adopted her.

"We have raised you as our own." Eva dabbed her eyes with a tissue. "And you want to repay us by taking away our income."

"The people come to see the others, too."

"Lorcan O'Leary the Living Leprechaun?" Eva snorted. "There are plenty of dwarves in the world. Noor the Rubberband Woman? Being double-jointed is not such a rare thing."

"There's Thea the Alligator Girl."

"A skin condition." Eva studied her reflection in a mirror beside the refrigerator, fixed her mascara, stroked some cherry lipstick onto her thick lips. Eva turned to Dusana and sighed. She began applying some foundation to her daughter's face and the sides of her neck. "I don't understand why these scars have appeared. You haven't been scratching your neck, have you?"

"Of course not."

Eva took Dusana's hand. "The webbing between your fingers seems thicker. Well," she added cheerfully, "thicker webbing makes the illusion more real, makes you unique." Eva rubbed some lavender scented hand lotion onto the webbing between Dusana's fingers. "The rest of the sideshows have mummified remains," she continued. "Chaloupeks' is the only sideshow with a real mermaid."

"But I don't want to be unique. I want to belong."

"You do belong, Dusana," Eva said and kissed the top of her blond wig. "You belong with us."

Before Dusana could answer, Rico arrived to assist her in getting to the tent and in place before the attraction opened to the public. "Morning, Dusie. Gonna be a hot one today."

"I'm melting already. This wig is killing me."

Rico's white teeth glinted. "Don't whine to a wolf-boy about July weather. At least your wig comes off at night. I'm covered in hair all the time."

Rico grasped Dusana's wheelchair handles and pushed her onto the porch, down the ramp, and along the walkway towards the pier where Chaloupek Brothers' Amazing Oddities shared the space with assorted games, street performers, rides, and food stalls. Rico whistled as they headed for the sideshow tents. He wore a tank top and athletic shorts; so most of people they saw stopped and stared at his fuzzy face, back, arms, chest, and legs. Dusana supposed they wondered what was wrong with her under her lap blanket. She felt like screaming, "Hirsutism. Sirenomelia." Instead, she smiled at the potential cash paying customers.

Rico patted her shoulder as they passed the string of hand painted banners that stretched in front of the sideshow tent. Their portraits were displayed along with the other Oddities. The wolf-boy on the banner-line was more fearsome than she imagined Rico could ever be; the mermaid who was supposed to be Dusana was perfectly formed, blond, and buxom; and the leprechaun was happier and sprier than the achondroplastic dwarf Dusana knew. The real Lorcan's foreshortened leg and arm bones were not designed for doing an Irish jig while playing the tin whistle—so he was always in pain. The rest of the portraits were also exaggerated versions of the sideshow entertainers.

The last character on the banner line was Thea. The alligator-woman's skin painted on the oilcloth was scalier and greener than Thea's flesh. Dusana knew Thea used an airbrush to apply jade makeup to her body, because her natural coloring was peachy-beige. Dusana used body paint, too, but applied her teal foundation by hand. Of course, she only used a small amount to blend her skin into the cloth costume's spangles, and lately, her fused legs had developed a bluish tint.

Eva told her it was because her veins were so close to the surface, but Dusana had her doubts. The skin on her legs was definitely tinged blue and felt cold, rough to the touch. Every night before she went to sleep, Eva massaged moisturizing lotion into the skin on Dusana's legs. "It'll be softer in no time," her adopted mother would promise. But it did not feel any softer to Dusana—if anything, it felt scalier by the day.

The tent flap brushing against her shoulder brought Dusana back to the present.

"Here we go, Dusie," said Rico as he lifted her from her wheelchair onto a scallop shell throne. "Some water and an apple," he added as he slipped a small thermos of ice water and a piece of fruit behind a Styrofoam branch of coral near her cushioned seashell seat. "I'll see you this afternoon for lunch." Rico waved and jogged out of Dusana's compartment towards the other end of the sideshow tent.

About five minutes later, Dusana heard Tomas begin his spiel on the bally platform. "Ladies and gentlemen, girls and boys, I challenge you to take a peek at Chaloupek Brothers' Amazing Oddities—but I must warn you, it is not for the faint of heart. We cannot be held responsible if you are shocked beyond words. We cannot be held liable if you suffer nightmares after witnessing the one-of-a-kind human oddities and anatomical wonders hidden behind these canvas walls...."

Dusana tuned out the rest of the bally talk. Instead, she thought about the letter she had sent to a hospital in London. She knew there were plastic surgeons there who could separate her fused legs, apply skin grafts onto the exposed tissue, and make her walk. Dusana often watched cable television specials that featured kindhearted doctors operating on the malformed for free. Her favorite surgeon, who had removed a huge tumor from a Mexican girl's face and fixed the crushed foot of a little boy from Thailand, was Dr. Bernard T. S. Smyth.

If Dusana could get a letter to Dr. Smyth at his hospital in London, she felt certain he would help her. When he said, "Yes," Dusana was sure Rico would help her get to the city. It would be easy to sneak away from Eva and Tomas after everyone was asleep. Then, Rico and she would catch a bus. Once they reached another town, they could get transfer tickets and head for London. When she was well, they would come back to the pier and together run a concession stand. She would wave to Eva in her ticket booth, hear Tomas giving his bally talk, provide extra change to Lorcan for his painkillers, and take special treats to her friends in the sideshow tent every day.

"And now, ladies and gentlemen, I give you a sample of the wonders to be seen in these tents."

Dusana shifted her weight, adjusted her sheer tail-fabric, and rubbed the scars on her neck. Tomas was giving the ballyhoo to attract a crowd. She shook her head as he continued, "Before you is Farid, The Amazing Pain-Proof Man. Not only will he lie down on a bed of nails, but one of you will be invited to stand on his chest…"

She didn't like Farid. There was something dishonest about him. Whenever he was around, Dusana had the feeling Farid knew things that she did not and was amused by her ignorance. She had no idea why Rico liked to hang out with him.

"Before you view the live exhibits," Dusana heard Tomas say, "take time to examine the rare specimens in the first tent. We have gathered these biological wonders from the four corners of the world. There are Frog Babies, Cyclops Babies, Lobster Babies, and—I hesitate to say this in front of the youngsters present—a Two-Headed Baby."

She heard the crowd gasp. Dusana giggled. Few, if any, of the specimens preserved in formaldehyde were ever living things. They were bouncers—fakes made of wax, resin, and even rubber. Last winter, she had carefully glued feathers onto a Styrofoam three-eyed owl to put in one of the jars, and Farid had cast a two-headed snake and a six-legged frog to add to the show.

Dusana put on her most alluring smile and pressed her music player's *ON* button as she heard Tomas exclaim, "Welcome, welcome. Chaloupek Brothers' welcomes all those who are curious of mind and brave of heart, all those who dare to study these mysterious freaks of nature."

The sound of terns and sloshing waves filled her under-the-sea exhibit. Dusana closed her eyes, and for a moment, she imagined herself perched on a rock in the ocean. Loggerhead turtles with bright green shells and brilliant tangerine starfish crept out of the salty water to keep her company. Cormorants, pelicans, and gannets filled the air around her with the flap of their wings and the plaintive music of their calls. Strange fish swam close, their dorsal fins slicing the water like little knives.

When the first patrons entered her tent, Dusana opened her eyes, moved her fused legs.

"Oh my, she really is a mermaid," said a woman with streaky platinum and gray hair. Dusana noticed her face was as tan and leathery as an old shoe.

"Jeeze, you can see right through that pantyhose thing she's wearing. Her legs are hooked together." The boy who spoke was just a few years older than Dusana.

"You mean like with straps or ropes?" a chubby girl holding his hand asked. "So you think she's a fake?"

"Yeah, she's a fake. Fake-o mermaid-o," joked a horse-faced boy.

"Stop it. You can see she's not a fake and," a girl with braces and curly hair pulled into two pigtails added, "she can hear you."

Dusana gazed at the teenager who had spoken. She was wearing knee-high boots with suede fringe. Attached to every third fringe strand was a silver disc. The discs looked like they had been hammered flat, then engraved by an Apache craftsman in front of his pueblo.

After Dr. Smyth fixes my legs, Dusana daydreamed, *Rico and I will visit the ancient Indian ruins and petroglyph sites in Arizona and New Mexico. Then, we'll go to a Navajo Reservation and watch the women weave their rugs. Next, we'll buy totem bags filled with pine needles, petrified wood, rattlesnake skin, and owl feathers from a roadside medicine man. Then, off we will travel to a honky-tonk bar somewhere in Texas where we'll straddle a mechanical bull and win first prize for staying on longer than anyone else.*

Dusana smiled. *One day after my surgery,* she thought, *I'll wear boots like those when I visit America. I will hike up into the Sierras, stir up some dust doing a Texas two-step with Rico, and stand on top of a mountain. I'll open wide my legs and ride a burro to the bottom of the Grand Canyon. I will learn to swim in the Pacific—kicking my feet up and down like one of those whirligigs that click-clack in the gardens of the permanent residents of seaside towns.*

"She's kinda pretty in a fishy sort of way," a man in his twenties told his friend.

Dusana remembered the customers, shook her head so the yards of artificial blond hair swayed and glimmered. She knew she was pushing the illusion, but the two men in their twenties seemed spellbound by a living mermaid.

"Move along, move along." Farid herded the last couple of gawkers into the next room of the sideshow tent. He paused in the doorway, glanced back at Dusana. "I think those two would take you home, Dusie. Then, what would Papa Tomas do?"

"He's not my real father."

"No, sweetheart, he's not. And he's not gonna want to change anything about this business, so you better get a grip on reality. The tourists want to see a mermaid who's with it—so focus on the customers, or they're gonna want their money back."

Dusana frowned. Farid did not know about her letters to Dr. Smyth, so he had to be talking about her daydreaming. She shifted position on her shell throne, rearranged her hair. Tomas and Eva might not be her biological parents, but they took good care of her. Loved her. When they saw her walking, thanks to the surgical skills of the kind and giving Dr. Smyth, they would be so happy that lost business wouldn't matter. Farid was a troublemaker, she decided, as she smiled and wiggled her legs at the next batch of show-goers entering her exhibit.

At about quarter-past-two, Rico walked into Dusana's part of the tent. "Got something for you." He handed her an official-looking envelope with a London return address. "I feel guilty rooting through Tomas and Eva's mailbox everyday," he said as Dusana tore open the envelope, started to read the letter it contained. "If this doesn't work out, maybe you should just let things be."

"This is it," she said. "I wonder when Dr. Smyth will want me to arrive in London. I bet I will have the surgery before the end of July. And I'll probably be back home, walking up and down the shore, by September."

Dusana began to read the letter. "Dr. Smyth and his associates say I'm an interesting case." Dusana lowered the letter slightly, continued, "But they need to see recent x-rays and doctors' recommendations before they can make a decision whether to take me as a candidate for surgery." The paper made a soft scraping sound as she folded the letter back into thirds, slipped it into the envelope. "And they need to talk to Tomas and Eva."

Rico shook his head, took Dusana's hand. "Eva will never agree to surgery, because you could die."

"But I want to learn to ride a bike, be free of this wheelchair."

"There are other doctors, other hospitals." Rico handed her a paper napkin from the lunch bag to wipe her nose with, squeezed her hand, and pushed a wayward hunk of wig hair from Dusana's forehead.

"They're all going to say the same thing. I'm never going to be normal."

"Who's to say what's normal? Look at me—I'm hairier than most, but I don't mind. I've got a job, friends here at the sideshow. So do you."

"But I'm never going to dance."

"Probably not." Rico kissed her palm, turned, and hurried to his exhibit.

Dusana rubbed her palm, thought about the warm furriness of Rico's cheek. He was always so kind to her—never failed to wave from the midway when he was hanging out with his friends or talk to her when he stopped by to visit the Chaloupeks. For the rest of the day, she thought about how she and Rico would travel to London after Dr. Smyth changed his mind and decided to fix her legs.

*I*t was just after ten when Chaloupek Brothers' Amazing Oddities closed its flaps. The last customers had oh-my-goshed and gee-whizzed their way through the tents, and Dusana and the rest of the sideshow crew were ready for a late dinner.

Silny usually helped Dusana into her wheelchair at the end of the workday and pushed her out onto the midway. It was up to Dusana how quickly she headed home. Most evenings, she sat for a while under the cobweb of lights and watched the carnival-goers wander by. The vendors gave her food samples, and the men who loaded the rides gave her free turns on the merry-go-round, Tilt-a-Whirl, Wild Mouse, Ferris wheel, and wooden roller-coaster. The merry-go-round was her favorite. It was so beautiful with its carved and painted horses, pigs, roosters, and rabbits. Dusana would sit in the stationary swan boat, listen to the calliope music, and watch the fabulous mounts bounce up and down on their poles. Someday she wanted to ride one.

But tonight, Dusana crawled to her wheelchair and climbed in before Silny or anyone else could come help her. She pushed the chair's wheels with her webbed hands and rolled to the end of the midway. She saw Rico and Farid strolling together towards a group of young men. They exchanged glances, and Farid slipped his hand into the back pocket of Rico's jeans. Dusana chewed on one of her fingernails.

She stared at the beginning of the Oddities Tent. Tomas was in the ticket cage with Eva. Dusana watched him sneak a kiss, and Eva push him away. But Eva wasn't angry—she was smiling and blushing. To their right, Noor had one of her rubber band arms stretched around Thea, and they were leaning on the side of a cotton candy and caramel popcorn concession stand. Their hips were pressed against one another, and they were sharing a cigarette. Noor whispered something in Thea's ear, and they both laughed. Behind them, Lorcan was using a cane to keep his balance as he tottled towards home.

Dusana imagined Tomas would come up with a new jig dancing leprechaun for next season. With some special makeup and a facial prosthetic or two, Lorcan would become a Fearsome Norwegian Troll or a Bloodthirsty Goblin from the Highlands, chained into place for the protection of the public. Carnival folks took care of their own. Tomas and Eva would never abandon Lorcan to government disability benefits.

Dusana rolled down the pier by the games of chance and under the pirate boat ride that swung out over the sea. It was nearly closing time, and the remaining people seemed to have broken off into couples pressed against each other in nooks and corners. She studied their feet. Some wore tennis shoes, some boots with fancy tooling, some sandals, and some spiky heels with their cute little toenails flaunting pink and purple and vermilion polish. She looked down at her own foot-like appendages barely visible beneath a nylon tail-stocking.

Dusana parked her wheelchair at the end of the pier. The calliope, rock 'n' roll, and big band music from the rides blurred into one glad anthem. From her jacket pocket, she withdrew the letter from the London doctors and shredded it into tiny pieces. The landward breeze lifted the bits of paper and sent them fluttering like gypsy moths towards the strings of lights. Dr. Smyth was not the right doctor for her. She would watch some more cable television specials and find another surgeon who worked miracles.

She gasped. The scars on her neck were throbbing. She touched them with her fingers and realized that her flesh had split open. She heard the air whistle in and out through the slits on either side of her neck just below her ears—ears that were ringing with the sounds of the sea lapping against the pilings.

Dusana climbed out of her wheelchair, crept beneath the railings, draped her fused legs over the wooden boards that stretched above the water, and balanced on the edge of the wharf.

She saw some beer and soda cans floating in the ship-wake from a passing fishing boat. She heard the gurgle of the ebb tide and knew now would be the perfect time to search the beach for shells and sharks' teeth. And as she smelled the saltwater filled with the tang of fish, waterlogged wood, and drowned things; Dusana remembered the feeling of belonging when the mermen pressed against her on the Ferris wheel in her dream.

And that is when she saw them, splashing in the night sea beside a pod of dolphins. The mermen had returned. Dusana—Mermaid of the Deep raised her beautifully webbed hand and waved. Then she closed her eyes, spread her arms, and leaned forward, ready to plunge into the water like an insomniac falling into a dream. In the distance, she heard Eva calling her name, but the wind tasted like the fish, and her fused legs longed to feel the caress of seaweed. Dusana opened her eyes, looked at the mermen. The moonlight spotlighted their pearly teeth and silvered their muscular torsos.

"Dusana, Dusana." Eva's voice was louder, more frantic.

Still the mermen beckoned, the sea wind pushed, and the seagulls jeered from the pier's pillars. And as Dusana teetered on the edge of the wharf, she felt large hands grab her waist.

"Got her," shouted Silny.

"Whatcha think you're doing?" Tomas asked as he reached Dusana. "Jeezus, Mary, and Josef." Tomas touched the gills flaring open and shut on Dusana's neck.

"Let me go," she begged. She saw the merman, one-by-one, disappearing beneath the Atlantic. "Please, let me go."

"Not so fast." Tomas licked his lips. "We've got ourselves a real mermaid here. I see television interviews, news reports, magazine articles, book deals…"

"And the most famous sideshow in the world."

"Hold tight to our mermaid, Silny. She's a precious commodity."

Dusana scanned the water's surface for the mermen. There was only one left. "You must let me return to the sea."

"Never," said Tomas as Silny lifted Dusana into her wheelchair, began to push her back up the pier towards Chaloupek's.

She looked back at dark water. The merman had vanished. She saw Eva running towards her with arms spread. Her adopted mother hugged her, crying.

"I thought I had lost you."

"Not to worry," said Tomas as he slipped his arm around his wife and smiled. "I promise, she's not going anywhere without us."

"Then, you must follow her to the sandy bottom," said a voice from behind them.

Dusana turned her head. There stood at least a dozen mermen. Their damp skin glistened, their wet hair hung down like black seaweed, and their eyes were darker than night.

"You just try to take her from us," said Silny as he slipped a knife out of his belt and stepped towards the merfolk.

"Wait." Tomas grabbed his brother's arm and pointed at the mermen's hands.

Two silver blades, curved and shiny as a crescent moon, were held by each merman. And as Dusana watched, more sea people climbed up over the edge of the wharf, blades clenched in their teeth.

"We have come to take her home," said one of the mermen as he stepped forward.

"No. Please stay with me," begged Eva. Tears gathered in the corners of the sideshow operator's wife's eyes. Her worn fingertips traced Dusana's jawline. Her brow furrowed. She inhaled quickly several times, then pressed the palm of her right hand to her lips.

"I can't," whispered Dusana as she reached out, stroked Eva's hair. "I love you, but I can't stay."

The mermen raised their blades. Tomas, Silny, and Eva stepped back as the merfolk moved forward. One of the mermen with a sea-star caught in his hair, smiled at Dusana. He knelt, lifted her up in his scaly arms, and without uttering a word, backed away from the Chaloupeks.

Then, Dusana, Mermaid of the Deep, pressed close to the cool chest of the merman with the sea-star in his hair. She gazed deep into his riptide eyes and returned his smile as they plunged into the water.

Selkie

We met on the beach:
you, with your soulful eyes,
and me, ready to believe.

With locked fingers,
we ran moon-speed
across the shell strewn shore,
climbed to a meadow
as green as a poem,

and on that plush velvet hill,
under a smashing, smoking sun,
you pressed your cold hands
against my flushed cheeks,
kissed me,

and I was forever
enchanted.

The Monks' Fosterling

*T*he trills and clicks of meadow wrens echoed about Brother Andrew, but he did not notice the bird sounds. In an attempt to keep his emotions in check, he instead concentrated on each rattle of cart, each pad of dog foot that carried him away from Clearflow Bridge.

"Foolish old man," he said out loud.

The pair of mighty canines that pulled his rig paused and glanced back at him.

"Sorry, pups," apologized the monk. For a split second, he considered turning the cart around and driving back to the toll bridge. But reason got the better of him, and Brother Andrew lightly flicked the reins and commanded the dogs to proceed forward.

Though the still air and afternoon sun of a too warm autumn day caused sweat to bead on his forehead, dribble from his chins, and darken his nappy robes, it was not the weather that bothered Brother Andrew. It was a terrible foreboding that he would never see Seamus, the lad he had help raise, again.

He and the other monks had done their best for the boy by securing the toll collector position on Clearflow Bridge after much negation with the Duke. It was a well paying job with a minimum amount of danger. In truth, there were limited opportunities for an orphan with no property, despite the fact Seamus was raised under the watchful eyes of twenty monks. Other than seafaring or soldiering, there were few honest occupations for a seventeen-year-old lad.

The monk rubbed his sleeve across his brow and shifted his position on the cart seat. The parting had been more painful than the monk had anticipated. He wished he was already back inside the walls of the monastery surrounded by the other Brothers. Though he knew they, too, would be in a melancholy mood.

But they had a right to their sadness. Seamus and his mother, Brena, had arrived on the monastery's doorstep fourteen planting seasons ago at the height of a storm. Through females were usually not permitted to stay at the stone retreat perched high on a cliff above the sea, due to the relentless rain, obvious poor health of the mother, and youth of the boy-child, an exception was made.

An apparent case of snowgrip had weakened the woman. Brother Andrew and the rest of the monks, moved by her frail beauty, had promised to care for her son until Seamus was grown. They had also promised never to allow Seamus into the ocean. An odd request for a sea town woman, even someone new to the area, but the Brothers had assumed Brena's husband had drowned while fishing or sailing on a schooner. A gesture of charity, the monks had labeled their actions, but quickly, the little lad had wormed his way into the heart of even the sternest of them.

The hooting of the evening's first owls reminded Brother Andrew of the late hour. He sighed, mopped his brown, and made a clucking sound. The dogs' ears pricked, and they hurried their pace.

The parting had been painful. Seamus shook his head and touched the beautiful Celtic cross on a silver chain that the Brothers had given him as a parting gift. He loved each of the kindhearted monks, admired them for their humble ways and service to the community. They had taught him to read and write, how to tend a garden, and simple healing methods. Although he tried not to dwell on his loneliness, his thoughts kept drifting back to the bustling stone monastery.

It had been three weeks since he had last seen his adopted fathers, and the Brothers were the only parents Seamus really remembered. None of the monks knew anything about his father. Not even his name. They had told him when he'd first arrived at the monastery, his mother had hummed sea songs and lullabies to him even as she lay dying. And he thought he remembered her voice.

Seamus scratched the back of his neck. He also vaguely recalled his mother's gray eyes, straw-colored hair, and smooth hands. And there had been something she'd whispered about his father at the end. But try as he might, Seamus had been unable to recollect what she'd said.

The rattling of an approaching cart and the rhythmic clop of horse hooves brought Seamus back to his duties. He hurried over to the waiting trader to collect the toll. After the coins were deposited in the metal coin box attached to the toll house, he lowered the bridge.

First, he turned the crank, then teeth caught teeth, cogs turned, chains strained, and the bridge lowered, then slammed. Next, the pony cart laden with barrels of bee-sweets, barley, and oats began to rumble across the planks, with Seamus ambling along side the nearest spotted pony, occasionally patting its rump. The cart's driver walked on the other side of the team.

"Been to Hartshorn of late?" Seamus inquired as they crossed.

"Aye, lad. I've just come from that sea town," the rot-toothed peddler answered.

Seamus could not suppress a smile. "Did by chance you see any of the monks? A Brother Andrew, perhaps?"

"Aye. I was in Hartshorn on Sabbath and visited the worship place to pay my respects. And your Brother Andrew welcomed all who came to hear the evening chants. A good friend of yours?"

"Aye, sir. A dear friend."

Seamus could almost hear Brother Andrew's deep voice greeting those who had made the climb to the monastery's chapel. Almost see the light filtering through the glass windows and illuminating the faces of the Brothers as they chanted songs of praise and thanksgiving.

"Of course, he has seen many winters. So there is no telling what the morrow will bring," added the peddler as he climbed back up onto the cart seat while Seamus held one of the pony's halters.

"I know he has lived a long life, but—"

"He ain't worm food yet, so be grateful for that," the trader said with a wink.

Seamus chose not to respond to the man's comment, through he was indeed grateful that Brother Andrew remained in good health.

"Nice speaking with you, lad."

"Good day to you, sir. And safe journeys."

The peddler grunted, jiggled the reins, and called to the pony team. After a few snorts and head shakes, the animals began to walk down the dusty road to Eggton.

Seamus gave a quick wave, turned around, and started back across the toll bridge.

The last three weeks as a toll collector felt like three months. Thankful for their years of care-giving, he wanted to please the Brothers. Wanted them to be proud of him. They had insisted he live in the outside world before allowing him to commit to a monastic life, and so he was trying to make the best of living in the stone house by the bridge, tending his vegetable garden, and meeting travelers. But he missed the rhythm of the monastery life, the evening vespers, Brother Andrew, Brother Calum, Brother John, and the rest of the monks. And he missed the sight of the ocean far below.

"Baa! Baa! Baa!

Seamus turned to stare at a small he-goat prancing across Clearflow Bridge. He glanced about the shoreline for its owner; instead, he saw two additional goats peering from between alder trees. The animals' pale eyes grabbed sunbeams and glinted with an eerie light.

"Go back, goat. Unless you want me to roast you for supper," joked Seamus uneasily. He tugged on his belt, located his dagger. The animals' otherworldly eyes bothered him.

The goat studied him, pawed the bridge, then spun around and trotted back to his comrades. The trio put their heads close together, and appeared to have a discussion as to their next course of action. After glancing over their shaggy shoulders at him several times, a consensus of some kind must have been reached, for a second goat clamored onto the far end of the bridge.

A bit larger than the first he-goat, the second creature was no less uncanny.

Knowing he probably did not have enough time to lift and secure the bridge before the goats could make it to the other side, he nonetheless vowed to prevent this trio from crossing to Hartshorn's side of the river. With as much courage as he could muster, Seamus frowned at the he-goat and stood in the middle of Clearflow Bridge with legs slightly spread and arms crossed over his chest.

"Go back, goat, lest you become my dinner. These fields," he gestured toward the countryside behind him, "Are no greener than the grazing land on your side."

The cloven-hoofed beast cocked his head, pawed the planks, but backed off of Clearflow Bridge and rejoined his friends. Another heads-together goat discussion ensued, after which the goats approached the toll bridge again.

Seamus's stomach tightened like curing leather as the three beasts marched up onto the wooden access ramp. This time, the third and largest he-goat moved ahead of the others, then strolled forward with his ghostly eyes gleaming like two full moons.

Though not an expert in local legends and dark tales, Seamus was positive shape-changers of an evil sort were trying to make their way to Hartshorn.

"Imps, bugbears, pucks, whatever! Return to your forest home," he ordered, then pointed to the woods on either side of the road to Eggton before adding, "I will not step aside and let you pass."

The goats bleated, then pulled their pink lips back to expose long fangs and carnivore teeth. They growled, lowered their heads, and charged. Seamus gasped, then jumped aside. But there was not enough room for him to avoid their lowered horns. The impact first knocked his breath away, then shoved him over the edge of the toll bridge.

Though the distance from the bridge to the water was little more than fifteen feet, time seemed to slow for Seamus. He felt like he was floating through the air, held aloft by prayers and unseen hands for several minutes. But eventually, the river won.

Water closed over his head with a chilly slap. He felt a prickly tingling like thousands of thistles were being pressed against his skin. His hands ached, and Seamus looked at them in the dimness of the river. Webbing stretched from finger to finger. Stroking his arms and kicking his feet, he was able to poke his head above water and breathed in the cool autumn air. Seamus felt his clothes slipping from his body. He glanced down and saw his skin was now gray and covered in fine hair. And where he expected to see arms, he now saw flippers.

Suddenly, summoned by the feel of the river water washing over his body, the words of a childhood conversation returned. He recollected his mother's voice whispering, "Selkie. I'm sorry, my Seamus, but your father was a selkie."

"Selkie?" he had repeated.

"A magical kind of seal that becomes a man when on land." She had stroked his hair. "You must never go in the sea, Seamus." Brena had added, "If you ever enter the sea, you will have to live among your father's people."

What his mother had not told him, or perhaps she hadn't known, was rivers that emptied into the brine were as powerful as the ocean itself. He glanced up at the goats. They were leaning over the edge of the bridge gawking at him with eyes wide, ears askew, mouths hanging open.

Aware the jabbing needle sensation had ceased, Seamus considered climbing from the river in seal-form in the hopes he would change back into a human once on dry land. But the banks on either side of the water were too steep to climb.

Brother Andrew, he thought. *Yes, the Brothers would know what to do.* He was sure the river where he now found himself emptied into the ocean not far from the monastery. So seeing no better option, Seamus faced downstream and began to swim.

*T*he peddler had witnessed the incident. He had tied his team to a tree and run back to the toll bridge, but the unnatural goats and lad were gone by the time he arrived. As he traveled from hamlet to hamlet, selling his wares, he told the tale of a toll bridge, three goats eager for greener grass, and a toll-collector who was never seen again. And weeks later, when he returned to Hartshorn, he drove his pony cart to the monastery and told the Brothers the fate of their fosterling.

Though no body was found in the river or along its banks, the Duke's record books listed Seamus's death as a drowning. In addition, the records indicated there was a significant increase in disappearances and unexplained deaths in Hartshorn and surrounding hamlets for several months following the drowning of Seamus, son of Brena, Monks' fosterling.

*H*eartbroken, Brother Andrew spent most of his free time by the sea. He sat on the rocks at the foot of the cliff on which the monastery had been built, and dozens of seals came up from the depths and surrounded him. Led by an especially friendly male, they always brought the monk an abundance of fresh fish which he dutifully carried up to the Brothers for evening meal.

The townsfolk of Hartshorn said nothing. Fisherman bobbing past in their boats said nothing. The Brothers gazing down from the clifftop said nothing. But all knew the truth. For each day when Brother Andrew stood at the edge of the water, he would call, "Seamus. Seamus." Then, the seals would pop their heads from beneath the waves and join the monk on the rocks. And always at the head of the pod was a large gray seal with a beautiful Celtic cross on a silver chain hung around its neck.

For the Good of the Settlement

The mirror cracked in 4252. Rue figured Granny Brigg's death and the Darwin Settlement Wars could be blamed on that crack. She had never replaced the glass. Rue wanted to remember the power of things. Things like mirrors and crows and bitternut trees deserved respect.

She stood in front of the flawed mirror, adjusted her wire-rims, and smiled. Though stained and sparse, Rue still had enough teeth to enjoy fresh-pulled corn. She rubbed her three front teeth with the side of her forefinger, then stepped back and picked up a battered hat from the dresser top. With movements as practiced as a dancer, she tied the bonnet on with a double-knot bow. Frowned. Straightened the offending head-wear.

"No sense in wearing a hat lopper-jawed, Halifax" she told a red squirrel balanced on the bedpost. The creature chattered a response and jumped to Rue's shoulder. She made kiss-kiss sounds at Halifax, smoothed her apron bib so it laid unwrinkled over her sagging bosom, fussed with a few white hairs that frizzed about her cheeks, and exhaled loudly. Rue turned from the looking glass and went through the living room to the kitchen.

Two more squirrels scampered around her feet as she flicked on the burner under the teapot. The trio of hyperactive mammals leaped to the counter top when she pulled a dented canister down from the wooden shelf above the sink.

"Here you are, dearies," she said, and poured a mix of hulled sunflower seeds, dried corn kernels, and walnut pieces into three small bowls.

She knew Halifax, Yukon, and Dodge did not like to share a bowl. Just like jealous five-year-olds, they would get into a quarrel, and she'd have to patch up the loser.

While her squirrels nibbled on their breakfast, Rue filled a tea ball with dried comfrey, dropped it by its thin chain into a mug, and poured boiling water from the pot into the hand-thrown drinking container. As she waited for the tea to brew, Rue stared out the window.

The morning sunshine filtered through the twisted branches of a bitternut tree. "Looks like a fine day," she told the huddle of squirrels who sat on their haunches and watched their caregiver. They tilted their faces up and gabbled. Rue bent and stroked their silky backs as their small spines arched in response.

The squirrels' fur reminded her of Mama. Mama had died from Bloodfly Fever when Rue was only eight. She had few memories of her mother, though she did recollect running her little-girl fingers through wavy, russet hair as Mama hummed sailing songs.

Rue didn't remember her father, a shipmate on the freelance freighter *Chancy Lady*, at all. Hort Vector had been knifed in a fight between planets, and his body jettisoned into space. And so she had been raised from age nine by her mother's mother. Though Rue never went cold or hungry, Granny Briggs was a hardscrabble woman with little need for affection, and no tolerance for slothfulness. As a result, Rue's childhood had been well ordered and unfeeling.

She pulled the dripping tea ball from her mug and set it in an enamelware bowl. Later in the day, she would empty the spent tea leaves out. After eight or nine tea ball's worth were piled in the bowl, Rue would take the dark grounds out to her Juneberry bushes. She knew the tanic acid from the left-over leaves was the secret to healthy berry bushes and flavorful pies.

Sweetened with just a sprinkle of dried stevia, she considered comfrey tea one of her favorite beverages. And though she would have preferred to linger in the kitchen relishing its bittersweet tang a few minutes longer, Rue knew chores waited doing. So she swallowed the last of the tea, set the mug in the sink, and headed for the backdoor.

"Come along," she called.

The trio whistled in response, and padded after her as she pushed open the screen with her good hand and stepped down onto the back porch.

The call of the rain crows from the thicket beyond the garden reminded Rue of the task ahead. She straightened her shoulders. Her back clicked three times. Rue winced, then thought perhaps cracks were like sneezes: three meant good luck. She glanced down. Squirrels wove between her legs and rubbed against her well-mended stockings.

She laughed at their antics and scolded, "Enough daydreaming. We need to be picking and cleaning today."

As if they understood, the squirrels led the way to the vegetables with Rue close behind. Rue peered at the suns' light bouncing off the pieces of scrap aluminum she had tied to the lima bean strings to keep the field hares from chewing the plants down to green nubs overnight. She did not hate the hares—they did what came naturally. Scrap aluminum, bloodmeal sprinkled around the perimeter of the garden, and diluted dog urine sprayed on the nearby grass dissuaded the rodents.

Natural annoyances were easy enough to deal with. But the intrusion of unpleasant and greedy people—that was a different story. She pursed her lips and thought about an appropriate curse for The Council of Federated Worlds. With their new interplanetary tariffs, the cost of seed had sky-rocketed. Not to mention even the local salvagers had been forced to raise prices.

With a duet of high pitched chirps, Dodge and Halifax tugged at the hem of her dress.

"Okay, dearies."

When Rue did not immediately begin the garden work, Yukon chittered and nipped at the toe of her shoe.

"Enough!" She laughed at her insistent squirrels, then started picking at the beginning of the first row of beans.

Even though she only had eight fingers, Rue was quick at manual tasks. She rarely thought of the wagon accident that left her two-fingers-short. Why, she considered herself lucky! Just last fall, Yates McGabe had lost both legs when his uncle's plow rolled over him. The Clinton Church of the Devout had held a Benefit Guinea Hen Fry and Auction to help collect enough credits to purchase a set of prosthetic legs for little Yates from the off-world traders who landed at Blacklake eight hours west of Clinton.

Rue had donated a handsome quilt that sold for more than 100 credits. The embroidery she had added to the patches had made the piecework spread a quick-sell. She glanced at the empty space where two of her fingers should wriggle. No use in mourning. Eight fingers served her fine.

Rue continued to pick the vegetables as Halifax, Yukon, and Dodge played a frenzied game of tag up and down the rows of beans. She didn't need to squeeze or pod-pop to tell which limas were ready. Decades of practice had taught her which beans were sweet to the tongue.

She looked up from her work and watched a squirrel swat at his reflection in a bit of shiny aluminum.

"It's yourself, Yukon," she said with a shake of her head. Then, after checking to make sure her bonnet was still tied tightly, she returned to her garden chore. She had finished harvesting the limas and moved on to the snaps when Violet strolled into her yard.

"Mornin', Auntie Rue. Want some help? Daddy told me to go find something to do while he worked on the roof."

"I'd be glad for your help. It will be good to talk to someone besides these old squirrels."

As if he heard her comment, Dodge jumped into Violet's arms. Rue grinned at the girl who was rubbing her face against Dodge's fuzzy back. She knew the grinning made her skin crinkle up so she looked like an quince-head doll, all leathery and wrinkled, with tiny black eyes peering out from behind her glasses.

Rue squinted, noticed the girl's left eye had been blackened, and there was a fresh bruise on her cheek. "How's your daddy doin'?"

"Okay, I guess," replied Violet as she tugged down one of her sleeves in an attempt to cover four ugly purple finger imprints on her forearm. The girl rubbed her face in the squirrel's fur again, then looked at Rue, and continued, "He stayed out late twice this week, and he's been real snappy. This morning he said if you weren't such a busybody, he wouldn't have to worry about me."

Auntie Rue frowned. "He said that, did he? Well, I'm glad I took you from your mama's stomach. Because if I hadn't, I'd have to pick all these beans myself."

Vi giggled, set Dodge on the ground, and began to help Rue pick snaps.

It irked Rue when she thought about Monty Hawkins. Instead of being thankful he had a daughter, he farmed Violet out to anyone who will keep an eye on her and complained about the woes of being a widower. Lately, thanks to corn whiskey, Monty was saying hurtful things to Vi. Just four days ago, he had told her the only reason he'd married her mama was that Sally had named him the father of the baby she was carrying.

Rue knew that Violet's mother, Sally, had come from Blythe. Monty had met her at a town dance and ridden his piebald gelding over to Blythe most every day for a month after that dance to visit Sally at the dry goods warehouse where she worked. Sally had confided in Rue one day when she stopped by to trade for some lemon balm tea that Monty had gotten her pregnant, married her, and brought her back to Clinton to live, only because Sally's father threatened to kill him if he did not do right by his daughter.

Rue shook her head, wondered if Sally had put her left shoe on first the day of her wedding—because she'd certainly had bad luck.

And it hadn't just been the marriage that was wretched. As if being wed to a mean-spirited man wasn't enough, the pregnancy had been rough. Rue had known from the beginning that Sally's marriage probably would not make it. Sally's father had been killed in a rustling incident just a month after the wedding, so Monty felt no pressure to be a good husband. He had made Sally work too hard, and left her alone while he went out hunting, rodeoing, and partying with some of the boys who frequented The Outlaw Saloon.

That summer thirteen years ago, he had been gone two days before Rue walked up the road to visit Sally, and see how she was doing. As she'd turned into their lane, Rue had heard a dog howling—a sure sign death was close. She'd hurried up the path to the Hawkins place. Sally had been in labor for more than a day. She was breathing real shallow and didn't know who Rue was. It had been beyond Rue's ability to save Sally, but she did save the baby.

Monty had come home the next day from a bull-riding competition. He was hung over from celebrating a second place win, and bruised and cut up from a brawl over prize money and some delinquent debts he owed to a local bookie. Monty had named the child after the barmaid he had been cheating on Sally with, thinking maybe she would come live with him and help out with the baby. She hadn't come. Rue and several other women from the church had ended up raising Violet.

"Auntie Rue."

"Yes, child," answered Rue as she returned to the beans.

"Papa tried to get into my room last night."

Rue frowned. "What happened?"

"The knob jiggling woke me up, but I had the door locked like you told me. I heard him loading and unloading his pistols, the knob jiggled again, he cursed, and then, it was quiet. He must have gone back to his room. He didn't say anything about it to me this morning."

"You just keep that door locked at night. Your daddy doesn't know what he is doing when he's been drinking."

"Yes, ma'am." Violet ran her hands through Yukon's fur, then asked, "Can we snap the beans and pop pods now?"

"Only if you promise to stay for lunch."

"Sure. Here, let me carry that basket to the house for you."

Rue's eyes narrowed as she watched Vi. She had bided her time waiting for Monty to sober up and treat his daughter right. Thirteen years. And not only hadn't Monty improved; he'd gotten more violent of late.

A shout from the front of the house hurried Rue's steps. Someone had stopped to buy her fresh cut zinnias, crocheted table scarves, rag baskets, and homemade jams and relishes. By the time she rounded the front hedge, Vi was waving at a one-horse buggy as it rolled away from the house. The big boned sorrel pulling the rig swished her tail and neighed, then, kicked up a cloud of dust as she trotted down the road.

"Look! He bought over twenty-two credits worth of stuff," Vi said as she rattled the tokens in her hand. "You live in the best place to sell things when it's not market day."

"Indeed, I do. Now, how about hurrying down to the root cellar for me and bringing up some more jars of preserves and jellies?"

"Sure."

After Vi disappeared into the house, Auntie Rue began to think about Monty again. She had watched him looking at Violet at the last Clinton Homesteaders' Pancake Supper. He did not look at her like a father should. When Monty had been over by the fireplace talking to some of the other men and making rude gestures, she'd told Vi to lock her bedroom door at night.

"She needs us now," Rue whispered to Halifax, Yukon, and Dodge.

The squirrels nodded their heads, clapped their paws, and winked as Violet came across the yard.

Rue adjusted her glasses and smiled a gap-toothed smile at the girl, "Classes will be starting soon, won't they?"

"Yes, ma'am."

"Your birthday is next week, and I'd like to take you to Ridley's to pick out a new outfit and some school supplies."

"Oh, Auntie Rue, you don't have to."

"I know, Vi, but I have been doing real well at the market stand this year, and you come over all the time to help me with the pickin' and cannin' and such. It would make me proud to buy you something special for your birthday. Just like your daddy says, if it weren't for me, you wouldn't be here. So I guess that makes me like family."

The girl hugged Rue. "You are family. I just wish I could live with you."

"I know. I know," Rue murmured as she patted Vi's back. She had asked Monty to let her have Violet for good about a year ago.

"You old hag," he'd jeered. "Why didn't you bed a husband of your own if you wanted a child? Oh, I forgot, crones lose their powers when they lose their maidenhood. Ain't that right, Auntie Rue?"

The other men sitting around the front of Ridley's had stopped talking. Though Rue had never done an unkind thing to any of them, she'd seen fear in their eyes. They all knew she tended the graves—venturing out in the graveyard after dark when the moons shone round and bright. Auntie Rue was the local wisewoman. Birth and Death were two doors. She helped open both of them for the residents of Clinton, Blythe, and beyond.

Rue had stood silent. The only sounds had been the buzzing of flies, the background hum of the power generator located behind The Outlaw, and an occasional *shoosh* as Frank Hughs spit tobacco juice into an empty molasses can.

"'Course if the price is right, I'm willing to sell her to most anyone," Monty had said, then elbowed Frank in the ribs.

A couple of the men had glanced at each other. Violet was right pretty, and Rue knew that most of them would have considered buying the girl if she hadn't been standing there. She had studied the face of each man loitering in front of the general store. One by one, they'd shaken their heads and looked at their boots. Finally, Rue's eyes had met Monty's.

"How much?" Auntie Rue had asked, staring hard at Violet's father until he'd begun to fidget.

"Too much for you," Monty had answered. "In fact, I would shoot her in the head before I'd sell her to the town busybody. So why don't you take your shriveled-up face somewheres else and leave us men alone." Monty had laughed and elbowed Frank again.

In a voice so quiet that the men had leaned towards Rue to make out all the words clearly, she promised, "Someday, you will wish you had given her to me."

Monty had shifted his weight from foot to foot several times, cleared his throat, and said as Rue was walking away, "You don't scare me none. A hard-favored woman like yourself ought to be nicer to folks, so when she's in need, somebody'll take pity and help her. But not you. You go around town threatenin' poor widowers and children."

Rue had kept walking. She'd heard Frank warn, "You'd better shut up, Monty. Auntie Rue is well-thought-of by most people around here." She had been too far down Main to hear Monty's reply.

"Come on, Auntie Rue," Vi called from the side of the house. "Let's go in and start on the beans."

"Lead the way, child."

*L*ater, after the lights in the nearby homes were dimmed, Rue went out to the herb garden and knelt in the warm soil. She shrugged off her nightgown and began to gather an assortment of plant parts from her medicinal shrubs and vines. The moons' light illumined her naked flesh as she chanted a harvesting rhyme from one of Granny Brigg's herb books.

"Moons' gift to wisewoman-kind:
root and weed, stem and seed.
I call upon the Olden One
to bless these gifts and give me powers,
for the need is great, and short the hours..."

Rue continued to chant as she collected the ingredients for Granny's version of skullcap tea. Luckily, Rue had plenty of madweed in the back corner of her garden, so the recipe's mainstay was at hand.

Though usually diurnal, Halifax, Yukon, and Dodge had gone to the herb garden with Rue. They burbled softly and crept over her skin clinging to its wrinkled paleness with their clever paws. Their small voices sounded like a chorus of children joining in Rue's harvest chant.

As Rue slid her arms back into her nightgown, a barred owl called from the bitterwood tree, "Who, who cooks for you?

The wisewoman chuckled. "I cook for Monty, but no one cooks for me."

With her squirrels perched on her shoulders, Rue walked into her kitchen carrying a basket of blessed plant parts.

The kitchen was filled with a noxious steam as she boiled the ingredients for skullcap tea. Tired and wanting to avoid the smell of the bubbling concoction, Halifax, Yukon, and Dodge scampered to their miniature beds and dreamt the night away as Rue worked until moons' set. When the day broke, she poured the distilled liquid into several vials and sealed them with corks and wax. One vial, she slipped into her crocheted shopping sack along with several jars of canned beans.

Rue, accompanied by her squirrels, went over to the Hawkins place around nine in the morning. She noted a rusted bale of barbed wire tangled in a harrow, several large pieces of jagged scrap metal, a broken pitchfork with its prongs pointing up, an uncovered well in the front yard, and bullet holes.

There were bullet holes in the side of the dilapidated barn, bullet holes in the fence boards, even bullet holes in the shutters on the cabin. She assumed if you swung those shutters closed, there would be slugs embedded in the logs underneath. Everybody needed a little target practice to keep sharp, so she had expected to see the usual gunshot-shattered bottles and hole-riddled tin cans. But this was different.

"He is giving us no choice," she told Halifax, Yukon, and Dodge. The squirrels gibbered their agreement.

"It is not something I enjoy."

The trio gabbled their understanding, and then, clapped their paws.

Then, it is decided, thought Rue. She forced a smile and hollered, "Hello. Vi? Hello in there."

"Auntie Rue?" Violet looked out the screen door. "Boy, am I glad to see you. Papa didn't come home again last night. It gets lonely here when there's no one around. Come on in while I finish picking up the kitchen."

The squirrels made squeaking sounds. "You three can come in, too," Vi added, then laughed as Dodge launched himself into her arms.

"Don't mind if we do." Rue stepped inside and looked around the cabin. Vi made an effort to keep things clean and mended, but the lack of money and repairs made the place look rundown. And the row of empty whiskey bottles lining the windowsill didn't help.

"Did you eat?"

"Yes, ma'am," Vi replied as she wrung out the dishrag and hung it over the corner of the fireboard. Dodge jumped to the floor from the girl's shoulder, raced around the room playing tag with his siblings. "I fried up three of the guinea eggs I gathered this morning and had them with some biscuits from yesterday."

Rue nodded. "Well, here are two pints of limas and two pints of snaps from yesterday's canning," she said as she pulled four jars from her shopping sack.

"Thanks. I'll run these down to the basement and be right back." Vi, followed by Yukon and Dodge, clamored down the cellar stairs.

"I will be waiting."

As soon as Vi was out of sight, Rue slipped the vial of skullcap out of her bag.

"Watch for her, Halifax," she said to her pet.

The squirrel sat at the top of the steps staring down into the basement as the wisewoman worked. Rue poured the vial's contents into a half-empty jug of whiskey that was sitting on the sideboard.

Halifax tittle-tattled and danced on his hind legs.

"Thank you, dearie," Rue whispered as she put the empty skullcap container back into her shopping sack. When Violet re-entered the kitchen, Rue turned to the girl and said, "Let's go to Ridley's and buy your birthday gifts."

"Okay, if you're sure you want to do that."

"I am sure, child. I am always sure of what I want to do."

They started back down the lane towards Main Street. Before they had gone far, the wisewoman clapped her hands and said, "Home, dearies. Town is no place for you three."

Halifax, Yukon, and Dodge yammered, then dashed up the lane towards their home.

Rue and Vi were nearly to Ridley's General Store and Emporium when Monty went careening by on his walleyed piebald. Startled by the horse and rider, a crow flapped up from the dirt street where it had been scavenging some spilled corn, and followed Monty cawing and cackling. Rue lowered her eyelids slightly and watched Violet's father gallop past without so much as a wave to his daughter. She shook her head, and then, followed the girl into the general store and over to the school supplies. They picked out two pencils, three pads of paper, and a gum eraser.

Rue pursed her lips. The skullcap brew she had dumped into Monty's whiskey was not deadly poisonous; it just made the drinker confused. After drinking a small amount, a person lost his sense of direction and his fear of dangerous things—things like narrow trails, loose rocks, steep drop-offs, uncovered wells, and guns.

They walked to the clothing section. Auntie Rue nodded as Vi selected a second-hand skirt, a flowery blouse, and two sets of under things.

Rue thought about Monty. It was a sin the way he neglected Sally. It was a sin the way he neglected Vi. It was a sin the way he used all his women. There were plenty of settlers who would like to see him gone. She sighed. Certain actions needed to be taken for the good of the settlement.

"Got everything you need for school? Remember, learning is the only way to better yourself."

"Yes, ma'am. Thanks, Auntie Rue."

Rue paid Amos Ridley the credits for the merchandise and watched Vi clutch the bag of clothing and school supplies. Violet and she exited the store and wandered by the stalls of the traders. She listened to the hum of conversation as settlers swapped produce, handicrafts, lumber, and aboriginal artifacts unearthed during planting season for the expensive off-world goods.

They spent several minutes rummaging through boxes of odd bits of machinery, appliances, motors, and such at Otto's Salvage, a stall near the corner of the street. Rue needed a replacement burner for her stove. She did not see anything that would do, but knew if you mentioned something to Otto he might just locate it on his next salvage run.

Rue spotted Otto watching them. She waved the trader over. "Have you come across any parts for a wood stove?"

"Not lately." Otto scratched his chin. "But I am headed out on a run next week, so I can keep an eye out for some stove parts."

"I would appreciate that," answered Rue. "I am especially interested in burners, but a few other parts could use replacing."

"You paying in credits or barter?" The trader had slid his hands into his pockets and was smiling a gummy smile at Rue and Violet.

"Credits, I think." She knew traders always preferred credits. And Otto was no exception.

Otto's smile broadened, showing even more of his pink gums. "I am sure I'll be able to find something for you, Miss Rue. By the first of next month, if not sooner."

"Thank you."

They departed Otto's Salvage and visited a few more traders' stalls. Rue was in no hurry. She wanted to be seen in town for several hours.

"How about a birch beer?" she asked Vi.

"Oh, yes!"

Rue smiled at the girl's excitement. "I believe we should be celebrating, and a cool glass of birch beer is the perfect way to do so."

"Celebrating my birthday?"

"Of course, Vi. What else could I mean?"

After finishing their drinks, they walked back to Rue's house for a late lunch. They canned some tomatoes in the afternoon under the watchful eyes of the red-furred squirrels. Rue heard the dogs howling around five o'clock. It was just past six when the sheriff rode up to Rue's place on his buckskin mare, leading a walleyed piebald with an empty saddle.

"Violet. Violet Hawkins. You in there, girl?" The sheriff called out as the horses trotted into Rue's yard.

Rue and Vi stepped onto the porch. The squirrels raced out the door with them, scampered up Rue's dress, and clung to the wisewoman's shoulders. Halifax, Yukon, and Dodge made rhythmic gurgling sounds deep in their small throats, flicked their tails like semaphores, and stared at the sheriff with bright eyes.

The lawman took off his hat, fiddled with its brim, and cleared his throat twice. "Violet, I got some sad news for you about your father."

As the sheriff explained the details of Monty's demise, Rue slipped her arm around Vi's shoulders and whispered words of comfort. Thereupon, three red-haired squirrels jumped to the ground, sat back on their haunches, chittered, and clapped their clever little paws.

At the Asian Art Center

Listen.
Hee-Young Kim has written
a poem
on four horizontal banners pressed
edge to edge like
river, grass, mountain, sky.

Look.
Strokes on these panels
translate odes
chanted by airy spirits
into the ear of Hee-Young.
And she, treasured interpreter, used
brush, paper, inkstone, and ink stick
to paint mementos of
the wind's meeting
beneath the Coincident Moon
with shy bamboo —
beyond graceful
in her robe of silvered jade.

Wait.
In this quiet, glass-and-wood gallery,
if you tilt your head, just so,
you will hear
the lament of owl
as she hides midst pine boughs,
and touch
the essence of abandonment.

Feathers

As they walked down the corridor to the last musty room on the left, the jailer hummed, and jingled the coins Thorn had given him. It seemed an outrageous sum to a potter, but Cutter refused to take less. And Thorn had to get into the cell that held the miller's daughter.

"Here you go, dwarf," said Cutter as he unlocked the barred door. "She ain't supposed to get visitors, but a half-man like you cannot do much harm."

Thorn ignored the jailer's jibe.

"Won't lock you in, just don't try to help the girl escape. Or," Cutter grinned and patted one of the knife sheaths looped on his belt. "Or I will show you how I got my name."

Thorn held his smile in place. Rather than a warning, the jailer's comment seemed a dare. He suspected Cutter would derive pleasure from slicing up a dwarf and a miller's daughter.

"Thank you for your assistance. I will lock the door when I depart."

The jailer nodded, hung the metal cell key on a nail outside the doorway, then strolled up the torch-lit corridor scrapping the stone wall with one of his daggers. Thorn waited until the rasp of metal against rock faded before turning around to face Rozlin.

"Why have you come?" asked the miller's daughter.

"To help," responded Thorn as he gazed at Rozlin. Her usually flawless face was puffy and red eyed from crying. Straw clung to her gown, caught in her dark hair, and was heaped in piles around her feet. Still, she was beautiful to him.

"No one can help." The girl sobbed. She tossed a handful of yellow stalks into the air for emphasis. "After a few too many pints, Father bragged I could spin straw into gold. The Sheriff overheard, and now expects me to live up to Father's words, or pay for his pridefulness with my life."

"That is why I have come—to spin gold." Thorn looked down at his worn leather boots, then lifted his too large head and gazed into the miller's daughter's pond-green eyes. "It is a thank you for the times you stopped the other children from tripping me and pelting me with horse dung."

"I do not think they realized how cruel they were." Rozlin tugged her dress's sleeves down to cover her wrists and straightened her spine. "They were young. Foolish."

"You were young, too." Thorn felt himself drowning as he looked into her eyes. He struggled to keep his head above water.

"True," Rozlin reached out and touched his shoulder. "But I figured we were both on the outs with the bullies. Me, with no brothers or sisters, and you, an only child, too."

"Friends. We have always been friends." The blood pounded in Thorn's ears. He needed air. "Though I wish..."

"Shush." She put her forefinger to his mouth. "There's no use in what-could-have-beens."

Rozlin froze, stared into Thorn's earth-brown eyes. She straightened her back again and resumed tugging on her sleeves. "I will hang tomorrow, because my father is a braggart, and the Sheriff wants to make a point," she said, and kicked the straw. "And that is the way of it."

"Not if the Sheriff finds gold here tomorrow morning."

"It is impossible."

"Some things are possible, whether you believe them to be or not." Thorn swallowed hard, stepped forward, and took her hand. He was cognizant of the continuous drip of water at the end of the corridor, the cooing of pigeons in the eaves, the pitter patter of mouse feet in the corner of the cell. Telling the truth turned out to be more difficult than he had imagined earlier in the day when he'd hatched the plan.

"I possess a gift from the Fair Ones. It held three wishes. One was used by my grandmother when she wished for a child. And I was delivered to her door." He winced. "Though I think she should have specified a perfect child."

"No one is perfect," said Rozlin as she squeezed his hand. "We are all flawed."

Thorn plunged forward. "I will use the second wish, and ask the Fair Ones to spin this straw into gold, so the Sheriff will set you free. But..." He paused. "But you must leave Bywater as soon as you are free. I think the Sheriff will want more gold, and find an excuse to arrest you again."

"Where would I..."

"We could go together. Through Huntsmen's Woods to another town. I can swap my cottage and land for a cart and horse. We can take my potter's wheel with us. And some household goods and..."

"You would give up your home and life here for me?" Rozlin's eyebrows were pinched together.

"Yes. As long as there is clay, I can..."

"I do not know if I believe the Fair Ones care about you and me..." Rozlin leaned forward. "But I do trust you. What do we do?"

Thorn exhaled loudly. He guessed he must have been holding his breath. "First, I need your ring to bribe the jailer should he decide not to let me leave."

Rozlin slipped the gold band with its tiny emerald off of her finger. "I will have little use for the ring if I am dead. Here."

He took the ring, dropped it into the pocket of his britches.

"Now, you must go to sleep."

"But..."

"I do not think the Fair Ones will come if you are watching."

Rozlin stood, brushed off her skirt, waded through the straw to a corner sleeping pallet, and laid down. "I am out of tears, and just about out of hope." She sadly looked at Thorn. "Should I be sleeping when you depart, good-bye, my dearest friend," said the girl as she turned her back toward him.

Faster than a minnow in the shallows, Thorn sat on the wooden stool vacated by Rozlin. He placed the spinning wheel in the correct position and gathered the straw around him. Next, he withdrew three feathers from his jacket's pocket and placed them at his feet. Then, he pulled the leather cord that hung round his neck from beneath his shirt. A whistle made from a thorny bit of wood dangled from the cord. He chanted in a whisper as quiet as the summer wind combing through grass, "Fair Ones, I need help this night to spin gold by scant moonlight." Finally, he blew on the whistle three times. Human ears heard no sound, but he knew he summoned help of the nonhuman sort.

An owl flew to the ledge of a barred window near the ceiling of the cell. It hooted softly, then silent as death, descended to the spinning wheel. As the bird stood motionless in the straw, a small woman in a pale gown slid off of its shoulder.

The Fair One surveyed the heaps of straw and glanced at the slumbering Rozlin.

"You wish to use a favor?" she asked as stroked her owl's feathers.

Thorn nodded.

"Does she love you back?"

"I do not think so." He looked down at his crooked hands. "How could she?"

"If you asked it of me, I could make her..."

"Thank you, but no. It wouldn't be the same," Thorn answered the Fair One as quickly as possible before he could be tempted. For he would be the happiest man in the world if Rozlin loved him.

The magical creature shook her head, made a sweeping motion with her arms, then turned her huge almond-shaped eyes to stare at the spinning wheel. She raised her hands and appeared to weave air as she chanted, "Petal pump and wheel spin. Turn straw to gold again and again."

When she was done, she picked up the three feathers offered by Thorn, and leaped onto her owl's back. "Sit and spin," said the Fair One. "But hurry, the blessing only lasts until first light."

"Thank you, Fair One. I don't know..."

"Hurry," she repeated.

Her owl clicked its beak and flapped its mottled brown wings. Thorn watched the two of them rise to the window, circle the room's ceiling several times, then soar into the night. Alone now with the straw and sleeping Rozlin, he focused his thoughts, and began the arduous task that lay ahead of him.

The mounds of straw glowed faintly, and as Thorn twined them, twisted them, and fed them into the spinning wheel, they turned to gold. Not coins, but strong metallic thread that could be loomed into the most marvelous cloth. A potter, not a spinner by trade, Thorn was grateful for the hours he had spent helping the local weaver. There would be none to compare to cloth woven from this golden thread—it would be shiny, glittering, and stronger than armor. He sighed. One never knew when life's lessons might prove useful.

It was moonset when Thorn finished the task set for the miller's daughter. He gave her reclining form one last glance, slipped out the door making sure to lock it behind him, strolled by the yawning jailer, and darted into a tunnel hidden by both architectural design and glamour. It was below the last set of stairs, and a tight fit even for a dwarfish man.

Cutter would assume he had entered and exited through the jail's street side door, having been questioned by the Sheriff's men. And that was exactly what Thorn wanted him to think. Non-human intervention required secrecy.

As he hiked in his lopsided gait through the underground passageway, Thorn mourned the loss of his goat.

Butterbits had faithfully provide milk to Granny Nona and him for years. Docile enough to harness to a cart, Butterbits was a prize. Which was why he was able to get so much coin from the weaver for renting her for one year. He sighed. The weaver and his wife had four young children, so the goat milk would come in handy. And if his plan succeeded, Butterbits would have a permanent home with kindly people.

He switched the lantern to his other hand as he neared the end of the stone tunnel. Granny Nona had shown him this passage once when they were in the woods gathering walnut husks for a golden brown dye to add to the clay they used to shape their pottery.

"I found it by mistake," she had explained. "But you never know when you will have need of such a place."

And, as usual, Granny Nona had been right. He only wished she was still alive to welcome him home, though he knew she would have wept at the loss of Butterbits.

Thorn stepped from the tunnel into the morning light. He extinguished the lantern, and cupping his hand to shield his eyes from the sun's glare, he trudged the half a mile or so through Huntsmen's Woods to the cottage he had shared with Granny Nona.

He hoped the Sheriff would be true to his word, and release Rozlin now that he had his skeins of metallic thread. But he knew you could never count on the goodwill and honesty of others. A childhood of harassment and ridicule had drilled that message into his head.

Before he stepped over the cottage's threshold, he glanced in the direction of town. Ten minutes walk down the road, the thatched roofs of the buildings on the outskirts of Bywater gleamed gold in the sunlight. And there on the edge of town was the mill that belonged to Rozlin's father and his brother.

*I*t was early afternoon when Thorn wheeled a load of mugs and pitchers into Bywater. Ordered by the owner of The Thirsty Hound, such mundane pottery was the bread and butter of Thorn's business. Nevertheless, he strove to add beauty to even the everyday ware that graced the tables of the common folk. Ostracized as a child, he had carved himself a niche in the town's heart with his fair prices and artfully decorated pottery.

He lowered the handles of the wheelbarrow, and wiped his brow with the back of his sleeve. Feathers were his secret. He found them when he gathered materials for his glazes. He found them when he dug clay along the riverbank not far from Rozlin's father's mill. He found them when he placed bowls and plates and mugs filled with goat's milk or blackberries among the roots of the massive oak tree hidden in the depths of Huntsmen's Woods.

"Gifts from the Fair Ones," Granny Nona would say when he picked up a feather.

"Watchful fairies or guardian angels?" he'd ask his grandmother.

"Does it matter? Perhaps they're the same," she would reply.

And Thorn had decided long ago that it did not matter. Perhaps fairies and angels were indeed the same. All he knew was a piece of pottery decorated using one of his found feathers always turned out well. Sometimes, he used the feather tips for brushing on glaze. Other times, he trimmed the spine and made a quill pen. He would then dip the feather pen in glaze, and use it to draw elaborate designs on his pottery. And, of course, he used found feathers to call upon the Fair Ones.

Thorn finally reached his destination. But before he could knock, the tavern-keep swung open the back door of The Thirsty Hound and motioned for one of his kitchen boys to unload the pottery.

"Don't want to miss the hanging," he explained.

"Hanging?" Executions were uncommon nowadays. Though Thorn had no interest in attending such an event, he knew many would show up for a hanging.

"The miller's daughter used sorcery to trick the Sheriff. So she is to swing in less than an hour."

Thorn could not catch his breath. He leaned on the side of the tavern for support. "Rozlin? Do you mean Rozlin?"

"That would be the one," answered the tavern owner. He counted out the coins owed to the potter. "Here, you go. I will have to place another order later. I don't want to miss the hanging."

"Where?"

"The gallows, of course. In front of the jail." The tavern-keep grabbed his hat and added, "You can come with me if you'd like. I..."

"No. I will go alone," called Thorn over his shoulder as he raced towards the jail. He scurried between animals, people, and buildings. If he had known earlier, he could have snuck in via the tunnel and tried to slip Rozlin out. Though Cutter or another of his kind would have made such an escape near impossible. As it was now, he would have to come up with a plan that could be implemented in front of the town's people.

Distracted by escape plans, Thorn nearly ran into one of the support posts of the gallows platform. An excited throng of on-lookers had gathered, and vendors peddling meat pies and sweets were hawking their wares. He craned his head and studied the execution apparatus. There were arms and nooses to hang five people, a large post with a metal ring attached for whippings, and a sturdy wooden block for beheadings.

Hands on his hips, the executioner paced at the far end of the scaffold. He wore a leather hood that hid his face from his mouth to the back of his neck. Eye holes had been cut in the hood and gave the hangman a frightening countenance. Beside the steps at either end of the gallows platform, stood a pair of guardsmen. Each guard not only held an eight foot spear, but carried multiple weapons. It was clear any attempt at a rescue would be met with deadly force.

Rozlin, garbed in last night's straw-covered dress, was already atop the scaffold with her hands tied behind her back. She kept turning her head and scanning the crowd. Even though it seemed foolish, he hoped she was searching for him.

Thorn hadn't had time to come up with an escape plan when the Sheriff, surrounded by four additional guards, strolled out of the jail. A hush descended, and the executioner stopped his pacing.

"Sorcery!" shouted the Sheriff in a voice more fit for a drama at the Bywater Playhouse then an execution. "This woman used magic in her jail cell to try and bewitch her way to freedom."

A murmur rippled through the crowd.

"There are witnesses," continued the Sheriff with a sweep of his arm. He beckoned one of the guards forward.

Thorn recognized Cutter. The jailer's face was bruised, his left eye swollen shut, and his nose obviously broken.

"True," said Cutter. "The miller's daughter called on the devil hisself. I heard her."

The Sheriff nodded, then gestured for Cutter to step back. "But there is more," he proclaimed as he slapped his gloves on the palm of his hand.

This time, two of the other men guarding the Sheriff came forward.

"We were beside the entrance to the jail all night," said the taller of the two. "No one came in or out."

"We was there until dawn," confirmed the shorter guard. "No natural person come through the doorway."

A mutter swept through the throng.

The Sheriff raised his arms, and the town's people gathered around the gallows quieted. "No one seen entering or leaving the jail, yet where there were once heaps of straw in this woman's cell, now there are piles of golden thread."

Gasps and shocked exclamations flooded the square.

"She denies sorcery, but when asked how this magic was achieved, she claims ignorance," shouted the Sheriff. "I say she lies, and deserves to hang."

A few bystanders in the crowd clapped.

Thorn glanced at the faces of the town's people. At first, doubtful of Rozlin's guilt, many now seemed ready to believe the miller's daughter dabbled in dark magic. There was only one way to save her—he had to take the blame.

"It wasn't Rozlin," yelled Thorn in the loudest voice he could muster as he limped towards the Sheriff.

"What did you say, dwarf?" There were deep furrows in the Sheriff's brow.

"It wasn't Rozlin, it was me. I called on the Fair Ones to spin the straw to gold. I wanted to save her life. I placed three feathers..."

Thorn's next words were swallowed by laughter. The Sheriff, the guardsmen, the crowd, even the executioner laughed.

"Go home, dwarf. Had you such power, I think you would be taller," mocked the Sheriff as he shifted his focus to the pending execution.

Again many in the crowd chuckled. They, too, had dismissed Thorn as a fool.

But Rozlin was not laughing. Instead, she studied him with glistening eyes and mouthed, "I will be fine."

"Hangman," commanded the Sheriff. "Proceed."

And that is when Thorn lifted three feathers in his right hand, blew three times on his wooden whistle that no human ears could hear, and used his last wish: "Fair Ones, rescue Rozlin, I beg thee. Please, save her. I ask nothing for me."

Without warning, the sky filled with owls. Dozens of barn owls with ghostly faces swooped around Rozlin. Hundreds of screech owls called in unearthly screams as they wheeled over the crowd. Countless great-horned owls flew at the guardsmen, hangman, and Sheriff. Just before they reached the men's faces, the owls swung their legs forward and tried to gouge out the eyes of their enemies with powerful talons.

Thorn stood still as a statue as the birds attacked. The town's people fled in fear and confusion, for most believed to see an owl in daylight was an ill-omen. The Sheriff and his men, preoccupied with protecting themselves from the winged onslaught, paid little attention to Rozlin. The hangman, who had been closest to the prisoner at the start of the ruckus, sprawled torn and bloody at the end of the gallows platform. And the condemned Rozlin was no where to be seen.

A large snowy owl sailed down and hovered for a spit-seconded in front of Thorn. Then, the bird reached out with one foot and snatched the three feathers from his right hand. At the same time, the owl grabbed the wooden whistle with its other foot, and tore the talisman from its leather thong.

"Go home," said the owl.

As if awakening from a dream, Thorn realized the danger he was in. Without a backward glance, he rushed to The Thirsty Hound and retrieved his wheelbarrow. Heart pounding louder than thunder, he hurried home. Once the wheelbarrow was back in its place in the pottery shed, he went into his cottage, pried up a floorboard beneath his bed, and pulled a tin box from its hidey hole. He opened the box, and removed the deed to his cottage and land. Swift as a spring stream overflowing with snow-melt, Thorn used ink and quill pen to scrawl on the document. He wrote that he gave everything he owned to the weaver, his wife, and their children.

Without pausing for food or drink, he ran to the weaver's home. Thorn handed the weaver the deed, saying only that he feared for his safety and would be leaving the area. He secured the weaver's promise to care for Butterbits until the end of her natural life, and gave the goat a last hug on his way back to his cottage.

Once home, Thorn packed a satchel with a change of clothing, a blanket, the money from today's Thirsty Hound delivery, his favorite book, a bit of food, a small pot, and two cups, plates, and spoons. He bundled his remaining feathers with a strip of cloth and slipped them into his pocket along with three coins. Then, he went to his potter's shed.

Thorn scooped a hunk of clay from a barrel. He kneaded the clay with powerful pushes and pulls. The brownish mud would look like a ram's head, he'd fold it together, knead again, and another ram's head would form between his palms. Over and over Thorn kneaded and folded the clay until he was satisfied there were no air bubbles hidden in it.

"Thank you," he whispered as he sat down and began to shape the three containers he would leave for the Fair Ones.

The drone of the whirling wheel was punctuated by the scruff of Thorn's boot kicking spinning stone. He hummed a farewell tune taught to him by Granny Nona while his thumbs opened the first mug's mouth. He loved to listen to each vessel draw breath and warble a birthing poem as he spreads its lips. One hand inside, the other out, he compressed the clay, gradually drawing his hands and the mug's sides up. The cylinder grew. Before the throwing wheel halted, Thorn lipped the pliable side of the container over his forefinger to give the mug a pleasing edge.

Once the kickstone was still, he sliced the first mug from the mound of clay. Singing softly, he carried the mug to his workbench and placed it on a wooden tray. Next, Thorn tugged a handle from some spare mud, pressed it into place, and smeared the two parts into a whole. He returned to the wheel and repeated the process.

Second mug finished, Thorn stopped working and listened. There were only the sounds of the woods. He rubbed his eyes with the back of his hand. There would be no running away with Rozlin, no chance of marriage or children or happiness. Thorn was, after all, an ugly dwarf who'd soon feel the wrath of the Sheriff. But at least Rozlin had escaped hanging. Somewhere, he felt certain, the Fair Ones watched over the miller's daughter.

For the final vessel, Thorn pressed a bit harder on the inside as the clay sides rose, and ended up with a rounder shape. After lipping the top edge, Thorn pulled a spout on one side. Again, he tugged a handle and attached it. Finally, two mugs and a pitcher sat on the tray. Rather than carry the damp vessels to his drying bench, Thorn readied himself to take the mugs and pitcher to the gnarled oak tree in Huntsmen's Woods.

He slipped on his cloak and loaded the travel satchel, feather bundle, a walking stick, a water sack, and the tray with the clay work into the wheelbarrow. He surveyed the pottery shed one last time. The glazes on the finished pottery shimmered and their decorative designs seemed molten as the last of the afternoon sun spotlighted his handiwork. He would miss this place, but in truth, it was the creation he'd long for—the metamorphosis of earth and water and fire into rock. That's where there was magic.

Thorn lifted the wheelbarrow's handles and trudged into the forest. Perhaps, on the other side of Huntsmen's Woods there was a town with clay nearby where he could settle. Perhaps. But there would never be another Rozlin.

Dusk made his journey through the woods treacherous. As he wove between trees and tripped over roots, he wished he had brought along his lantern. But Thorn knew it would have been near impossible to hold the lantern and push the wheelbarrow at the same time. Owl light would have to do.

Night had fallen by the time he stumbled into the clearing by the ancient oak where, like his Granny Nona before him, he had regularly left gifts for the Fair Ones. He lowered the wheelbarrow and flexed his fingers. They were stiff. He massaged his hands for a moment, took a deep breath, and unloaded the newly made pottery. Next, he placed one coin in each mug and the pitcher. He also dropped Rozlin's ring into the pitcher. Cutter had not asked for any more payment, and Thorn could no longer return the ring to its rightful owner. Giving the circle of gold with its tiny emerald to the Fair Ones seemed fitting. Then, he divided the feather bundle into three parts and placed a third in each of the vessels. Lastly, he tied the strip of fabric around the pitcher's handle.

"I will always be grateful to you for saving Rozlin," he said as he backed away from the tree. "I leave these..."

Thorn's next words never left his mouth. A snowy owl like the one from the gallows landed on the ground by his pottery. The creature inspected the gift, ruffled its feathers, turned its head, and studied him with its dark eyes. The dim light made it difficult for Thorn to see clearly what happened next, but where owl had been a moment before, a woman dressed in a feathery gown now stood. He bowed his head, believing this must be a Fair One.

"We have watched over you since birth. Since you were left by this tree. Since we gave you to the potter and his wife," she said.

And as Thorn lifted his over-sized head, he saw there were now eight other women in the grove. Each wore a gown that glimmered in the rising moon's light. Each had kind eyes. One held a mourning dove nestled in her hands.

"We saved Rozlin as you asked by transforming her into a dove," explained the Fair One who had first appeared as the snowy owl. "But alas, we cannot change her back to a woman."

Thorn leaned forward and stared at the mourning dove cradled in the second Fair One's hands. It gazed back at him with pool-green eyes.

"Now, we give you a choice." The Fair One who had appeared first as an owl smiled and touched his cheek. "We can keep Rozlin with us until her time is over. Or you can take Rozlin with you, and care for her yourself. Or," she paused, tilted her head. "Or we can transform you into a dove, too. Then, you can spend the rest of your life with her."

"Lady, what does Rozlin want?"

"Always putting others first." The Fair One shook her head. "Not to worry. She leaves the decision to you."

He chewed on his lower lip. He had been willing to die so Rozlin could live. Now, he knew he was willing to forfeit shaping clay, speaking, reading, writing, and his human form for a woman who had never loved him.

"If I may, Lady," he said, and turned to face the mourning dove with the green eyes. "Rozlin, if you will have me, I'll change to dove-form, and we can spend our lives together."

The dove cooed and fluttered to Thorn's shoulder.

"Then, it is decided," said the Fair One who'd first appeared by the old oak in owl-form.

The nine Fair Ones circled Thorn and Rozlin. The maidens lifted their shining hands, sang a hymn of earth and sky, and in the moment of silence after the last chorus beneath a moon as round as a clay bowl they knelt.

Thorn felt weightless—like he was in a dream. He looked down to see he was covered in gray feathers. *Rozlin*, he thought.

I am here.

He turned his head in the direction of the response. A mourning dove with green eyes took several steps towards him.

You chose me, thought Rozlin. *And now, I choose you.*

And with those words, Thorn and Rozlin flew to the lowest boughs of the ancient oak tree.

He did not know how many days or months or years they had together—but for Thorn, it was enough. And he swore to himself, to Rozlin, to the Fair Ones who were quickly fading into the shadows of the forest, and to the far-flung stars that he would never abandon his beloved.

Henkie's Fiddle

Stirred by a bone-chilling wind, the lone tree in the unsanctified section of the cemetery rattled its bare branches. Duffy had the eerie feeling that Witchman's Oak sensed what was to happen today. He chewed on the hard skin left by a burst blister on his right thumb and studied the tree.

By order of the Edgewater town council and with the mayor's approval, Duffy was to remove Witchman's Oak before Christmas despite local lore proclaiming the tree haunted. Personally, he thought it was a terrible mistake to cut down the oak if for no other reason than the shade it provided in the summer. Rousted by another cold gust, the huge iron bell hanging from a rusted hook embedded in the tree's trunk clanked its agreement.

Duffy felt the hairs on the back of his neck rise and glanced around—nothing but grass, grave markers, fence, a few birds, and cloudy sky. He shook his head. He may have been a superstitious gravedigger and cemetery caretaker, but he was not an ignorant man. In fact, had his grandfather left him any money when he died last spring, Duffy would have started college this fall. Instead, he had taken over his grandfather's job and cottage. Perhaps it was not the future he'd dreamed of—but he had steady work, food on the table, and could retain ownership of the cozy stone house he had grown up in.

And so, out of curiosity and for a bit of mental stimulation, Duffy had decided to learn more about Witchman's Oak. Before the mayor had even signed the tree's execution decree, he'd gone to the local Historical Society to locate information on the solitary oak in Edgewater's potter's field. He had discovered an account of a man accused of witchcraft who'd been hung in the town square. According to entries in the diary of one of Edgewater's founding fathers, after the hanging the witchman had been sealed in a casket with a four-leafed clover, three daisies, a sprig of St. John's wort, and a branch of mountain ash. Then, the coffin had been hauled to the cemetery. Once there, bread and salt along with a bit of churchyard mold had been scattered over the casket. Next, the burial box had been covered with dirt and sprinkled with water from a baptismal font. Lastly, an oak tree had been planted over the grave.

Another tattered document stated that years later, a stout iron hook had been hammered into the witchman's oak and a bell secured in the crook of the hook. And there was a faded paper that forbade any other grave or disruption of the sod for twenty-one feet in all directions.

The bell clanged again as Duffy pulled the starter on his chainsaw. The mayor and town council were penny pinchers. That unfilled ground in the middle of the pauper's section of the cemetery looked like a waste to them. Once the oak tree was gone, he had no doubt they would find a way to charge a fee for burying the poor and unidentified in the newly available space. He swept his sandy-colored hair out of his eyes, crossed himself just in case, and began the task of cutting down Witchman's Oak.

As he sawed, a murder of crows gathered and perched on the three rail fence that surrounded the unmarked grave portion of the Edgewater Town Cemetery. Fastidious creatures, they preened their glossy, black plumage then polished their beaks on the fence rails. Later, when Duffy took a water break, he heard the corvids cawing in raucous voices. He was not sure if they were shouting: "Cut. Cut. Cut."

or "Halt. Halt. Halt." Either way, the bird's intelligent eyes studied him with unnerving intensity.

While he'd been using the saw to notch all the way around the oak's wide trunk, the clouds had thickened and the temperature had dropped. Though only late afternoon, with the heavy cloud cover, it was growing dark. Today was the winter solstice, and the season seemed to be arriving on schedule. But December or June, Duffy had a job to do. So without further delay, he pulled his work gloves back on and cut horizontally into the south side of Witchman's Oak.

The tree shivered. Duffy pulled the chainsaw away from the trunk, stepped back. The oak groaned, and then the top of the tree tumbled to the ground with a harsh knelling of iron bell, a loud tearing of wood, and a ground-shaking thud. The crows flapped their wings and screeched, but refused to abandon their front row seats for the tree's removal.

Duffy looped a thick chain around the severed trunk, attached the two end links to his tractor, and hauled the gnarled treetop to a refuse area at the rear of the graveyard not far from the caretaker's cottage. Once he'd unhooked the chain, he attached a small wagon to the rear of the tractor and chuffed back to the stump. He had turned off the tractor and climbed down from its seat to load up his tools for the day when the ground began to tremble.

As the earth quaked violently for about thirty seconds, Duffy was knocked to his hands and knees. And it was from this vantage point that he witnessed Witchman's Oak's stump split. Then, four of the roots from the north side pulled up from the ground and tore a chunk of the stump with them. Duffy could make out the shape of an over-sized calf in the animated root-stump. The beast snorted and shook like a wet dog. Dirt and debris showered down on the ground and the still prone Duffy. As the rest of the oak stump lifted up, the animal lowered its head and glowered at him with malevolent eyes.

Before Duffy could get to his feet, a bearded, shaggy-haired man wearing a gray shirt and pants sprang from the hole left by the uprooted stump. With a motion as smooth as the swing of a baseball bat, the man in gray pulled an ax from his belt, jumped to Duffy's side, grabbed him by his shirt collar with impossibly big hands, and pressed the ax blade against the skin of Duffy's neck.

"Name!" ordered the man in a gruff voice.

"Duffy Irwin."

"Irwin?" The bearded man removed the blade from Duffy's throat and yanked him to his feet. "Stand up, lad. 'Tis time to prove if your bloodline is a worthy one."

"I'm not sure what..."

"Have ye still the bow and fiddle?"

Duffy was tongue-tied. The wild looking man before him was gently stroking the huge stump calf with one hand and picking dirt from between his teeth with the forefinger of the other. Thankfully, the nasty-looking ax had been returned to a loop on the man's belt.

"Are ye daft? Answer me, lad."

"Yyyes," stuttered Duffy. "I have an old violin and bow at the caretaker's cottage. They've been wrapped in a cloth bag and stored in back of the closet for..."

"Generations and generations," finished the bearded man. "Henkie Trow," he proclaimed grasping Duffy's hand and shaking it vigorously. "Spooty, my faithful buggane, and I will not harm ye if the fiddle and bow are still intact," Henkie said as he patted the black calf, then pushed Duffy in the direction of the caretaker's cottage.

"To my knowledge they are in good condition," responded Duffy as Henkie and he walked. He noticed that his companion had a pronounced limp, but thought it best to not mention the problem. Duffy also noted Henkie was broad shouldered, barrel chested, sharp toothed, and extraordinarily hairy. Fear quelled Duffy's curiosity about the cloven-footed buggane trotting beside them—he refused to even glance in its direction.

"Of course, I have never really tried to play..."

"And wise it was to never play a trow's fiddle." Henkie smiled a toothy smile. "I suppose I would have to use my ax on ye, laddie, if you had plucked a tune on Henkie's Fiddle."

Duffy shook his head. "I am not musical at all, sir."

"Sir!" Henkie chortled as they reached the front door of the cottage. "Stand watch, Spooty," he added with a wave of his hand. "You may consume any who approach." The bearded man turned to Duffy. "Invited me in, lad, and show me my fiddle."

*I*t took what seemed like hours to Duffy for Henkie to meticulously examine his bow and fiddle and proclaim the instrument unharmed. He tried to sit unnoticed on a bench near the fireplace, but his guest's glittering black eyes monitored his every movement. When Duffy scratched his nose, Henkie lifted his head and watched. When he tilted his head back and forth a few times to try to release some tension, Henkie pursed his lips and peered in Duffy's direction.

"Darkness," said Henkie Trow in a voice loud and deep enough to make Duffy jump. "Darkness, yuletide, ax, bow, and fiddle are all that are needed for settling a blood debt. Of course, a buggane eager to wreak havoc is a bonus." Henkie chuckled and began to sharpen the blade of his ax.

Duffy's eyes widened. He looked at his guest, but dare not speak.

"My name is not Henkie Trow, though you may call me by those words," said the bearded man as he continued to sharpen the ax. "I am indeed a trow, a being of faerie-kind. Trows rarely choose to initiate trouble with men, but we will not back down from a fight."

Henkie rubbed his elongated thumb along the ax blade. Nodded, then spoke. "Trapped, but not dead I have been. Locked by plants and such in an earthen prison. Luckily, plants decay and men forget. Once the iron bell was removed by you, laddie, Spooty and I were free as birds."

As if on cue, Duffy heard a tapping at the window. There on the other side of the glass were the crows from the graveyard. He scanned the room. Feathery faces with bright eyes were pressed to glass panes in every window.

"Spooty and I lived by the river when the first men arrived," explained the trow. "They named their settlement Edgewater, and soon coveted the land by the riverbank where I resided in a small green hill. I was happily tending my gardens and playing my fiddle when they plotted to take what was mine."

Henkie stomped his feet. The whole cottage shook. "Charged I was with witchcraft. A trow with witchcraft!" He scowled, then looked at Duffy.

Unsure how to respond, Duffy shook his head and did his best to appear shocked by the very thought of a trow charged with witchcraft.

His expression of dismay and outrage seemed to satisfy the burly trow who resumed his tale. "Four liars told untruths. A dishonest judge found me guilty and sentenced me to death. And then, those five foolish men took possession of my land and gold." Henkie wagged a finger in the air, then ran it across the front of his throat like a dagger. "Five foolish men who turned a friendly trow into a haggersnash."

Duffy was not certain what a haggersnash was, but he was certain the word had to do with anger and revenge.

"Are these families still bullying the people of Edgewater?" asked Henkie prior to rattling off five surnames.

Duffy could not suppress a gasp. The trow had named the mayor and four members of the town council. Their families were the wealthiest and most powerful in the county. "I do not want to get anyone in trouble, sir. There are some people with those..."

"I can locate the villains myself," said Henkie as he stood. "But to make certain your kindheartedness does not get the best of ye, I will be keeping you in eye-shot. Grab your coat, lad of Irwin blood, for tonight you ride the winter wind astride old Spooty."

Ignoring his protests, Henkie dragged him out the cottage door. Bow and fiddle in hand, the trow leaped onto the rough back of the oak tree buggane, leaned down, grasped Duffy under his arm, and swung him up onto Spooty, too. No sooner had he landed on the malformed calf's back, then Spooty shot into the air. Afraid of tumbling to the ground below, Duffy wrapped his hands around Henkie's waist. The trow howled, the buggane flew faster, and dozens of shrieking crows flapped alongside of them as they skimmed above the housetops. Duffy squeezed his eyes shut as they neared the mayor's home.

The buggane's hooves had hardly touched the ground, when Henkie hopped off the shape-shifting faerie creature. But hard as he tried, Duffy found himself unable to dismount. Spooty swung his head around and gave him a warning glare. Duffy stopped struggling, and sat quietly on the oak calf.

Henkie tucked his fiddle under his chin and drew the bow slowly across the strings. The crows, who had alighted in the nearby trees, laughed. Then, the trow began to play a fast paced tune. The spritely notes poured from the wooden instrument with such speed and sweetness, that Duffy felt lightheaded. From the corner of his eye, he saw the crows begin to move about on the limbs of the trees like black suited dancers. Had he been able to climb down from Spooty, Duffy knew he would have been compelled to dance, too.

Within seconds, the back door of the mayor's house swung open. Out waltzed five men—each holding a handful of playing cards in one fist and either a bottle of beer or a glass of amber fluid in the other. Duffy remembered it was Saturday night, so the mayor and his councilmen would have been gathered for their weekly stag night poker game.

A twisted grin spread across Henkie's face as he played faster and faster on his violin. The trow nodded at Duffy and the buggane, turned towards the river, and began limping his way to the mayor's boat dock. The mayor and the councilmen twirled and two-stepped their way across the lawn and down the path behind the fiddling trow. The crows, still laughing and moving their thin legs in time with the music, flew above them. With a snort, Spooty trotted after the enchanted parade.

Still unable to dismount, Duffy had a sparrow's ticket to whatever was to happen next. And as Henkie stood on board the mayor's boat wielding his magical fiddle, Duffy knew it was not going to be pretty. And it wasn't.

As soon as the mayor pirouetted onto his boat, the trow struck him once on his head with the broad side of the ax. The mayor dropped like a stone to the deck. Henkie repeated the process with each of the four town council members. When the descendants of the five foolish men who condemned the trow and stole his land and wealth sprawled unconscious, Henkie took his ax's blade and slit each man somewhere on his body.

After the blade had tasted the blood of the five men, Henkie nimbly hopped from the boat to the dock. The crows, who now danced on the dock's planks and pilings, cheered. While chanting in a language that Duffy did not recognize much less understand, the trow hacked a large hole in the vessel's starboard side. Whistling a shrill tune, the trow next untied the boat and shoved it away from shore. As she drifted out into the current, Duffy saw the words *Money or Nothing* painted boldly on the boat, and shivered.

Suddenly, the trow resumed fiddling with renewed ferocity. Fish of all sorts jumped upward from the dark waters of the river. They twisted in the air, mouths opening and shutting, then fell to the water with a cacophony of loud slaps and splashes.

About fifty yards offshore, the *Money or Nothing* was sinking rapidly. His smile now stretched to grotesque proportions, Henkie did an awkward jig while still playing his fiddle, then stopped playing. The silence that followed was louder than the music had been moments before. The trow gazed directly at Duffy, again made the knife-across-the-neck motion with his forefinger, then pointed at the mayor's half-submerged boat.

"Eat!" shouted the trow in a voice that rumbled like snow thunder.

The murder of crows lifted into the air and winged their way to the *Money or Nothing's* deck. The thousands of fish swam to the vessel and surrounded her with a ring of shimmering, squirming, scaled bodies. As the feeding frenzy continued, the buggane rose up on its hind legs. Spooty whirled around, snorted, and bellowed in a most uncalf-like manner. When Spooty stopped dancing, Henkie jumped onto the buggane's back in front of Duffy.

"Away! All debts but one are paid," shouted the trow.

Duffy held tight to Henkie as they zipped into the air, soared over the treetops, and eventually alighted in front of the cemetery caretaker's cottage. He tried not to think about the mayor, the councilmen, the crows, and the fishes. But he had a feeling the grizzly demise of the five men would haunt him for the rest of his life. As he slid to the ground, Duffy noticed it was beginning to snow.

"Inside, laddie," urged the trow. He opened the door and nudged Duffy. "Keep watch, Spooty," he called over his shoulder before stepping into the cottage.

Duffy stumbled across the room and flopped down on the hearthside bench. He put his head in his hands. No matter how tightly he squeezed his eyes shut, he could still see the flashing silver of the fish as they fought for a taste of the mayor and councilmen. And who to tell? No one would believe a tale of a trow and buggane out for revenge.

"Let it go, lad." Henkie patted his shoulder. "Ye could not save those who owed the faeries a debt."

Duffy raised his chin, met the intense gaze of the trow. "But I wanted to save them just the same."

"It is done." Henkie yawned, stretched his arms over his head. "Now, Henkie and Spooty must return to the Greener Forest. Duffy Irwin, can you hold your tongue and keep faerie secrets?"

Duffy studied the still-bloody ax on the trow's belt and Henkie's black, nothing-but-pupil eyes. He nodded. "By the time the authorities find the boat and whatever remains of the bodies, the deaths are sure to be classified as accidental. I have no evidence that contradicts that assumption."

The trow patted his shoulder once more, then stood. "As payment for faithfully guarding Henkie's fiddle and bow, those of Irwin blood will always be faerie-blessed. And for freeing my buggane friend and me, ye are welcome to whatever hides below this hearthstone." Henkie stamped his foot on the edge of the flat stone in front of the fireplace. The stone flipped up to reveal a hole filled with gold coins.

"'Tis faerie gold, but it is real—not glamour."

Without further comment, the trow strode to the door and flung it open. Spooty snorted and shook off the coating of snow that covered his back. Henkie climbed onto the buggane and smiled one last time at Duffy.

"Laddie, choose whatever future suits ye," said the trow. "But do not be too hasty to leave this cottage—for there is more than one secret buried in potter's field."

Before Duffy could respond, Spooty spun round and galloped westward towards the thick forests of a game preserve. Though the falling snow obscured his vision, he thought he saw Henkie raise his violin to his chin. And then, Duffy Irwin, faerie-blessed cemetery caretaker and rich man would have sworn he heard the lilting strains of a fiddle tune.

The Pinnacles

The mountain goat romp up sandstone
saturates my tee-shirt.
A deer-fly, attracted by sweat, hovers overhead
as I climb the boulders whose surface
feels warm and alive beneath my fingertips.
Finally on top of the rock formation,
I survey miles of mountains, canyons, buttes —
but I did not come for the view.

Local inhabitants claim this knob is haunted,
make warding gestures when uttering its name.
Sitting on its stony peaks,
I, too, feel a presence.

I gulp some water
and regret not having purchased a bottle
of herbal tea from the town's New Age Cafe.
Perhaps after a sip,
the power of spring water and mint leaves
gathered in the dark of the moon
would have allowed
my dream-eye to glimpse the structures
whose ruins I tread.

I doubt earth shifts created this place.
I concede rain has rasped edges rounder, smoother;
centuries slipping by have cracked, crumbled;
and stunted shrubs attest to winds
that have snapped, whittled;
but it was humans—ancient, long-gone humans
who measured, molded, and carved these forms.

And there are humans—ancient, long-dead humans
whose shades still wait here.

On a Midwinter's Eve

Beneath the scant shelter of a spruce, Brock paused and wiped snow from his eyes, cheeks, nose, and mouth. The weather had taken a dangerous turn not long after he'd departed the cabin, and he now found himself calf-deep in drifts with no dinner bagged. Bagged? He snorted out a cloud of warm breath as he resumed his search for a deer. He had brought no bag. Anything he managed to shoot would have to be carried on his broad back or flung on a pine bough and dragged home.

And why the sudden longing for venison? He had rarely hunted with anything more deadly than a camera these past five years. He was, after all, a researcher paid by others to find background information for magazine articles, books, genealogy projects, and such who had grown to love a comfortable apartment life.

In fact, it was a fluke that he was even at the cabin. After his dad's death earlier this month, Brock had decided to move his computer, work files, book collection and other belongings to the log structure. He had inherited the building and the land it stood on, free and clear, so he was saving a wad of cash by staying here. And he had all he needed: internet access, mail delivery, electricity, indoor plumbing, a working well, phone service, and a store not too far away.

But ever since he had heard the persistent calls of a barn owl last night, the well-stocked pantry and full freezer seemed inadequate.

He could think of nothing but deer meat. And when he thought of the smell of venison roasting over the fire, he actually found his mouth filled with saliva.

Therefore, after this morning's coffee and oatmeal, he had hauled several loads of firewood from the shed to the cabin's porch, double-checked the supply of kerosene for the emergency lanterns, and unpacked a couple of extra blankets from the cedar chest. He knew the telephone and electric lines strung up the mountainside from the road might be damaged by the weight of the predicted ice and snow, and wanted to be ready just in case. When the storm preparations were completed, he had searched through the contents of the attic and located his old crossbow.

He looked at the bow in his right hand. A gift from his father, Brock had used it to take the life of at least a dozen bucks over the years. He shivered, pulled his knit cap down lower on his head. He did not like to think of those venison steaks and burgers as former deer. It was easier to think of them as meat that arrived packaged and labeled from the butcher's shop.

To his left, Brock heard branches breaking. He froze. He needed to stop musing over past hunts and focus on the task ahead. With eyes narrowed, he scrutinized the swath of forest where he thought the snaps had emanated from: tree trunks, boulders, snowdrifts, debris, and a bit of brown fur visible beneath the drooping branches of an evergreen tree.

Fur! Arrow notched and ready, Brock raised his bow in slow motion. Determined to be as stealthy as a fox, his shallow breaths seemed to shatter the quiet. Just as his finger began to squeeze the trigger, a pale owl dropped from a branch above him and snatched the wool cap from his head.

Surprised, he yelped and swatted at the creature. Then, afraid the bird might return to grab more than a knit hat, Brock lowered his bow, crouched down, and searched the gray skies for the owl.

It was not long before he spotted the creature. It was perched on a gnarled oak branch, glaring at him.

"What's it to you?" he called to the bird.

He was not worried about frightening away game. Any respectable deer would have bolted at his first surprised shout.

"It was bigger than a mouse. And I am just as hungry as you are."

"Kschh! Kschh! Kschh!" responded the owl.

Brock would have felt better if the creature had hooted at him. The owl's eerie rasping hiss combined with the bird's dark eyes boring into his eyes made his heart pound. He recognized the bird as a barn owl by its heart-shaped face. Perhaps it was the same creature which called outside his window last night. But why would it follow him into the forest? And where was its nest? He had been spending time at the cabin since boyhood, and knew of no barns or other buildings this deep in the woods.

"And where is your home? I might have need of it if this storm continues."

Again the owl hissed, "Kschh! Kschh! Kschh!"

"You are useless. I cannot understand a word of your chatter. So, go your way, and leave me to my hunt. That deer can't have gotten too far."

"Then, can you understand me, Hunter?" said an elderly woman garbed in a tattered robe as she stepped from behind the evergreen with the sagging branches.

Brock gaped at the woman. Below her hood, her face had turned blue from the bitter winds and freezing temperatures. It was the most severe case of frostbite he had ever seen.

"Ma'am, we need to find you shelter. See if we can warm you up." He glanced down at her bony fingers protruding from ragged sleeves. They were even bluer than her face. "And I don't think there is any time to lose."

The woman cackled. "I would be more concerned about your safety than mine." Then, she gestured with her staff toward a rock outcrop. "There is a cave over there."

For a split second, Brock felt the urge to flee in the opposite direction of the old woman's cave, but the howling of the wind had increased to blizzard levels. Any shelter at this point would be better than staying out in the elements, besides the woman obviously needed whatever first aid he could render. And so he followed her, slogging his way through the drifts, and hoping there was a spot to build a fire inside the cave.

"In here, Hunter," said the elderly woman as she ducked under a low shelf of rock and vanished into a opening between two boulders.

Brock followed. After traversing a narrow passageway, he found himself in a large room brightly lit by lanterns and candles. There was a fire crackling on a stone hearth at one end, two wide wooden benches covered with blankets and pillows at the other, and a table and several crude chairs in the middle of the room. The cantankerous barn owl was comfortably roosted on one of the chair backs, still clutching Brock's knit cap in its talons.

"I would like that returned," he said, and took several steps towards the bird.

"Kschh! Kschh! Kschh!" The owl tilted its head and appeared to laugh at him. Next, the bird used its hooked bill to pull a thread out of the cap. It paused, eyed Brock.

"Apologize, and he might give it back," suggested the blue-faced woman.

"Apologize!" Brock glanced at the barn owl. The bird tugged the thread again, looked in his direction, and opened its beak.

"Okay. I am sorry I was trying to shoot your deer friend for my dinner. Can I have my hat back?"

The owl lifted up, flew to Brock, and tossed the cap into his hands. As the bird returned to the chair back, Brock noticed its legs were long and its wing feathers were tawny with a few cinnamon and gray patches on them. The bird's fluttery wing-strokes reminded him of a pale summer moth, even though it was the dead of winter.

"Thanks."

The owl nodded.

Suddenly, Brock remembered the frostbitten woman. He shifted his gaze to her, only to find she was studying him with pursed blue-black lips. "What foolishness sent you out on winter solstice at owl-light?"

"Owl-light?"

"Twilight, then," said the crone as she removed her robe and tossed it on one of the benches.

The long ice-blue sweater and bluish white dress she wore beneath the robe were worn and oft-patched. On her feet, she wore heavy black boots, and around her neck draped a necklace with a large colorless stone dangling from its center. Her hair was twined in a long gray braid and her eyes were black—so black, it seemed to Brock that they were all pupil.

But it was her blue skin that shocked him. That was until he recalled reading about a man from the western part of the United States who ate a little bit of silver everyday in the belief it made him healthier. He had turned blue. Granted it was a grayer blue than the woman before him, but the man had turned a shade of blue because of silver consumption. Since the woman's blueness did not seem to be causing her pain, Brock supposed the old lady had also ingested silver over a long period of time.

"Call-yak," said the blue-faced woman as she went to the fire, lifted the lid of a black pot, and stirred its contents.

"Excuse me?"

"You may call me Call-yak. Would you like a plate of stew in lieu of a deer?"

"Well..." Brock rubbed his chin. To take food from a stranger was not something he would usually consider, but he was famished. If he did not know better, he would have thought there was a tapeworm gnawing away inside his belly. He studied the woman's face again. She seemed a little younger and a little less blue.

"Yes. That is, if it is not too much trouble. I could use a plate of stew. And my name is Brock. I am sorry if I was rude just now, but..."

"The skin color surprised you." Call-yak finished his sentence. "Few people know what to expect when the moon is waning and the North Wind howls like a wolf."

The word *wolf* had barely been uttered when a white wolf padded into the room, calmly looked at Brock, and went and curled up by the fire. Call-yak glanced at the wolf, smiled, and handed Brock a plate of stew and a spoon.

Brock backed to one of the chairs, pulled it out, sat down opposite the barn owl, and dipped the utensil into the thick stew. He wondered again if it was safe to eat, and delayed actually tasting the concoction by stirring and blowing across its surface.

Call-yak dished out a second plate of stew and placed it between the paws of the wolf. The great beast gave Brock a look of disdain, and proceeded to gulp down the vegetable mixture.

"Is the stew not to your liking?"

There was a challenge in Call-yak's voice. A voice, Brock noticed, that was less filled with the rasp of old age then a moment earlier.

"Would you rather have deer?" she queried.

As she said the word *deer*, three does strolled into the room, trotted over to the blanket-draped benches, and knelt down. The three bowed their heads to Call-yak, then lay like obedient dogs beside the sleeping benches.

The owl, who had managed to keep his thoughts to himself until now, chortled, "Kschh! Kschh! Kschh!" Which now sounded to Brock quite like, "Witch, witch, witch!"

Seeing no out, Brock ate a spoonful of Call-yak's stew. It was more delicious than anything he had ever eaten. He gobbled up the contents of his plate, but felt more ravenous then before.

"More?" asked the blue-faced woman as she ladled out another serving of stew with hands now smooth and young-looking. And it seemed to Brock that her clothing was not quite as tattered as he had first thought.

Again, Brock cleaned his plate. And as he finished the last spoonful of the vegetable stew, he realized that Call-yak's braided hair was now black as her eyes and her ice-blue gown and sweater now flowed around a younger, curvier body. He squinted. The blue-faced woman's skin was wrinkle-free and her lips seemed fuller and strangely seductive.

He agreed to another refill. The barn owl flew over to the table and stood by Brock's plate. The owl raised and lowered its head with every mouthful he consumed. And its eyes seemed bright with intelligence. He turned to make a comment to Call-yak about the sentient owl, but found himself unable to speak.

Call-yak's ebony hair tumble down her back and around her shoulders. Three braided silver chains with blue and clear jewels attached crossed her brow and wrapped around her head like a delicate crown. At regular intervals, long strands of silver chains bejeweled with the same blue and clear crystals dangled among the locks of her hair.

"More?" said the stunningly beautiful Call-yak.

He nodded and held out his plate for a refill. After the fourth plateful of vegetable stew, his belt felt too tight. Brock loosened the offending leather strap and buckle, and gazed longingly at the black kettle. He was a big man, solid and muscular, but another helping of dinner would never stay down.

"A glass of milk to top it off?" Call-yak's melodic voice encouraged as she poured milk from a pottery pitcher into a mug. Brock saw there was snow still clinging to the outside of the pitcher.

"That sounds perfect," he replied as he grasped the mug's handle and drank the chilly liquid. "I do not believe I have ever tasted better milk," he began. "I guess it is because..."

"It is deer milk," finished the woman whose head dress now included a cluster of white feathers on either side of her head. "For the deer are my cattle, the wolves are my dogs, and this owl is my dearest friend."

Too full to stand, Brock merely raised his arms, then let them fall into his lap. "I did not know. Honestly, I meant no offense it's just that I was..."

"Hungry?" Call-yak laced her delicate blue fingers together. "Are you hungry now?"

"No, but…"

"No." The enchanting maiden with the pale skin, tinted ever so faintly blue, strolled over, leaned down, stared into Brock's brown eyes with her black pupils. "From this day forward, you will never taste of animal flesh. Should you put so much as a crumb of meat into your mouth, you will change into your namesake."

"I don't understand."

"Brock," stated the woman, "is the Old Ones' name for a badger."

"Badger!"

"Indeed." The woman used a fingernail to trace a symbol on his forehead. Before he dared ask what she was doing, Call-yak explained, "Rune. I have traced a binding rune upon you, Brock, Badger of a Man. Henceforth, you are a friend and protector of animals and a servant of Cailleac Bhuer."

"Who is…"

"Call-y'ac V'fhoor?" the woman said with a twisted smile. "'Tis I, Daughter of the Winter Sun, Ancient Fairy of Midwinter, Protector of Deer and Wolves. Some call me Blue Hag, some Stone Woman, some Goddess. I am all of those things, and none of them."

Brock frowned. "Was the old woman from the forest your true form? Or is the young-looking woman before me now, really you?"

Call-yak laughed, a lovely laugh that sounded like small birds singing and the ice-encrusted branches of a fir tree tapping together. "Neither, Badger-Man. They are both glamour."

The fairy cupped his chin in her cold blue hands. "And would you stay with me if I were the beauty before you?"

He did not know how to respond. A part of him wanted to nod his head and stay with the Protector of Deer and Wolves. But another part of Brock wondered what sort of creature was hidden by the glamour.

The Ancient Fairy of Midwinter smiled. "Someday, Badger-Man, you will indeed see my true form, but not today." Then, she clutched the crystal orb hanging on her necklace, and continued, "You have eaten of fairy food and will crave it always, but do not search for this cave."

Before Brock could respond Call-yak snapped her fingers and the pale owl flew to her shoulder. She whispered something to the bird, and it clicked its beak in response. She snapped her fingers again, and Brock finally felt himself able to stand.

He rose slowly, a little unsteady on his feet. A sudden thought crossed his mind. He had spent time in a fairy cave, and legend said that time flowed at a different speed in Faerie.

"How much time have I lost?"

"Not long," answered Call-yak of the pale skin, dark hair, and snowy gown.

"Will the world have changed so much I cannot recognize it?" Brock asked. He was afraid of the answer.

The fairy shook her head. "Only a week has passed outside this cave, and badgers are fond of spending much of the winter underground."

Brock ignored the badger comment. "Thank you for your hospitality, Call-yak," he said as he edged towards the cave entrance.

"It is because of your lack of aggression towards my owl and your concern for my imagined frostbite that I showed you hospitality. But tread carefully, Badger Man. Next time, I might not be in such an amicable mood."

The wolf trotted over, stood to the left of the beautiful fairy. The deer rose, clip-clopped to the right-hand side of the Daughter of the Winter Sun.

"My owl will lead you to your cabin. Keep your eyes on him and do not look back. A single glance over your shoulder, or a single word to anyone of what has transpired here, or a single bite of animal flesh, and you will find yourself on all fours wandering through the world in badger-form."

"You have my word that I won't..."

"I do not need your word," responded the Daughter of the Winter Sun. "My spells are strong."

Brock pulled his slightly damaged knit cap on his head as he took another step in the direction of the entrance. "Will I see you again?"

The blue-faced woman shrugged her shoulders. "My friends will watch you always, and I will peer through the trees in your direction whenever the North Wind blusters and snows fall at midwinter." Then, she added as the owl flew from her shoulder, "Especially if the moon is waning and it is owl-light."

As instructed, Brock kept his eyes on the barn owl as it flapped out of the cave into the predawn twilight. He thought he heard the Daughter of the Winter Sun, Ancient Fairy of Midwinter, and Protector of Deer and Wolves call, "Fare-thee-well, Badger Man," as he neared the edge of the forest, but he dared not respond.

And when he saw his cabin in the distance, Brock was acutely aware of four things: the eerie, "Kschh! Kschh! Kschh!" of the ghostly owl overhead, the heaviness of his bow, the eyes of hundreds of woodland animals locked upon him, and a terrible longing to return to the cave of Call-yak.

Kingdom Across the River

As mice run helter-skelter
through this place of forgetting,
it is forbidden to speak of clocks
tick-tocking the hours away
or mention almanac dates
gobbled by a greedy man.
Here, daffy-down-dilly never
brings spring to town in
gaudy gown and petticoat.

No bell horses ring one, two, three
in this realm of quietude,
and it is taboo to listen for the tolling
of church bells on the hour
or acknowledge the gray donkey
braying for the dawn.

In this land of half-light,
it is a crime to count the grains of sand
trickling through an hourglass.
And residents are discouraged from
peering across the river,
marking the phases of the moon,
and checking to see if the old woman
has swept the cobwebs from the sky.

An owl hoots eight times
for sudden death,
pauses, then hoots six times more
for guests arriving
as the boatman whispers,
"Hush-a-bye, hush-a-bye,"
and paddles the new arrivals to the dock.

"No need for rhymes or lullabies," he says.
"You are safe forever
in the realm of the dead."

Bells

The hundred and fifty-year-old Crosby family farmhouse on the corner of Park and Millstone Streets was cluttered with the dead. What should have been gray-toned or sepia photos of Melinda's ancestors peered from shelves, tabletops, curio cabinets, and almost every available inch of wall space. But the pictures of the deceased had not been left in their original neutral tones—in an attempt to add life to the images, her Great-Aunt Vivian had garishly tinted the people's faces, clothing, and surroundings with photographic oil paints. But by blessing men, women, and children with red lips, rosy cheeks, and brilliant irises, Aunt Viv had given everyone in the pictures the same unnatural appearance that was found on corpses at an open-casket viewing.

The room in the house on the corner of Park and Millstone where Melinda always stayed when she came to visit, had belonged to Aunt Vivian's mother, Isabelle Worthingham. Mel glanced at her Great-Grandmother Belle's augmented photo on the marble dresser top. She shuddered. If she braided her waist-length coppery hair and pinned it to the top of her head in a bun, Mel would have been a dead-ringer for the long-gone Isabelle.

She touched the elaborately filigreed frame. Mel could almost hear her great aunt promising in her most wishful voice, "The dead are only separated from us by the sheerest gauze."

Mel pressed her lips together, lifted her gaze from her great-grandmother's picture, leaned forward, and checked her mascara for smudging in the wavy glass mirror. Standing behind her and just to the left, Mel thought she glimpsed the blurred image of Isabelle Worthingham. She gasped and turned around. There was no one else in the room, only the bed draped in a shooting star quilt made by Belle, golden oak furniture laden with Belle's carefully preserved belongings, the ever-present photographs, and a profusion of evergreen branchlets tucked here and there around the room.

Melinda stepped over to the window, watched the snowflakes sail down to the sea of white that covered the lawn, the sidewalks, and the cemetery across the street. Considering the weather, it was lucky most of her mother's family still resided in the same town where their parents and their parents' parents had lived, died, and were buried. Other than Mel and her sister and parents, everyone coming tonight for Christmas dinner could walk home if need be. She pulled the lace curtains together as far as possible trying to shut out the wintry scene below. But there was a bundle of greens tied together with red ribbon and bells dangling from the center of the rod, so not only didn't the curtains close all the way, but her effort at privacy set off a metallic jingling.

Shaking her head, Mel crossed the room to the bed, closed her suitcase, then strolled into the hallway. After a quick turn to the right, she descended the winding stairs to the main floor. The ghosts seemed to press less closely there, or so she thought, until a chill brushed past her on its way downstairs.

The aromas of a roasted turkey and honeyed ham on the counter awaiting slicing, sauerkraut with pork chops simmering on a stove burner, rolls baking, and pumpkin and minced meat pies cooling on the buffet added to the sharp scent of the pine and spruce decorations. Before Mel could sneak past the kitchen to the living room where the first batch of her cousins were noisily arriving, Aunt Vivian spied her.

"Melinda," called her great-aunt with a wave of her mitted hands. "Come here, and help carry the food out."

"Sure," she responded.

There was no use fighting the inevitable, cheerfully or begrudgingly she was expected to help out. *Cheerful seems a better idea on Christmas*, Mel thought as she struggled to weave her way through the bustling kitchen. Granny, Mom, Cousin Helen, and Aunt Viv's best-friends Olivia and Lillian were each busily putting the finishing touches on one dish or another.

Lill handed Melinda two potholders, pointed to a baked bean casserole. "Take those out first." The old woman gave her a gummy grin.

She has forgotten to put in her teeth, again, Mel thought.

"Then," Lill added with another toothless smile, "hurry back for the dressing."

She returned Lill's smile. She liked her great-aunt's short, chubby friend from across Park Street. Lill had frizzy white hair that refused to obey bobby pins, an amble bosom with lots of cleavage which she used as a convenient spot to tuck a pack of cigarettes, a raspy voice, and a contagious laugh.

The penalty or reward, depending on the point of view, for being the eldest female cousin among the Crosby, Dare, and Kent clans was that Melinda at age seventeen was expected to help out in the kitchen while her little sister and half a dozen male cousins watched television, played cards and dominoes, worked on puzzles, and read old-timey picture books. Still, it made Mel her great-aunt's favorite—and it was nice to be someone's favorite, especially at the holidays.

The extended family's adult males had gathered in the parlor to discuss sports, the weather, car repairs, the drive-time between various destinations and Vivian's house, and of course, good times past. They all appeared to be engaged in spirited discussions except for her Great-Uncle Clay. Uncle Clay in his green holiday sweater with the red collar and zipper, sat in an armchair in the corner of the room with his eyes closed. He had been recently widowed, and she supposed today was hard for him.

As Mel surveyed the room, she saw only one woman with the men: Aunt Lena, Melinda's mother's brother's wife. Uncle Fred and Aunt Lena had no children, which seemed to make them hold tighter to each other than most couples. Lena's fruitcake was already on the buffet table—sliced and decorated with red and green candied cherries. And Fred and Lena had also brought wine for the adults and fancy candies for the kids. Besides spice-flavored gumdrops and peanut brittle, they'd brought chocolate-covered raisins and cherries, fudge, caramels, and the foil-wrapped strawberry hard-candies that had a soft center.

Mel's gaze was drawn to the front door as the Christmas carols blaring from the television were drowned out by a cacophony of bells. The jangling of sleigh bells along with the clank of a large cow bell heralded the arrival of the last of her cousins. As the late comers added their mufflers, gloves, hats, coats, and boots to the heap of outerwear hung and piled in the foyer, she considered the door bells.

Before Mel was born, Aunt Viv had hung a leather strap full of bells along with a cow bell on the inside knobs of both the front and back doors of the house on the corner of Park and Millstone. Her great-aunt believed they were better than a burglar alarm or barking dog at dissuading would-be thieves. The bells sounded festive and appropriately seasonal tonight, but Mel knew they tinged and clinked every time someone entered the house whether it was the Fourth of July, Easter, or December twenty-fifth.

"Melinda, pickles!" called Olivia from the kitchen.

"Be right there," she responded as she nearly tripped over the edge of a braided rug on her way through the dining room. As she passed the table, she saw the flames on one of the candelabras waver, then extinguish, almost as if someone had blown them out. She shivered. There was no draft in this room and no one else passing through but her. Melinda picked up the box of matches, emptied a match into her hand, scraped its head across the roughened box bottom, and re-lit the three still smoldering candles.

"Leave them burning," she whispered over her shoulder to the gallery of relatives watching from the wall as she stepped from dining room into kitchen.

While Mel scooped the various home-canned pickles from glass jars, she surreptitiously studied her great-aunt's friend, Olivia. Even with Vivian's photo tampering, Olivia was lovely in all the old pictures. Years later, the seventy-plus year-old woman wielding a potato-masher with confidence in her aunt's kitchen was still attractive. And Olivia was an excellent cook—famous locally for her cakes, pies, jams, and pickles. But neither she nor Aunt Viv had ever married. Nowadays, they spent so much time together they seemed more sisters than friends. They permed each other's hair, shared most meals, and in fact, once every three weeks, split a bottle of strawberry-blond hair dye to touch up their roots.

Her Good Cook reputation is well-earned, thought Mel as she popped a watermelon pickle in her mouth before carrying the plate of pickled peaches, cucumbers, cauliflower, carrots, onions, peppers, and watermelon rinds to the dining room table. From the corner of her eye, she thought she saw the curtains move and a shadow slip behind their fabric. The hair on her arms rose, but she did not bother to examine the draperies. Mel shook her head—there was no sense in looking. She was certain she would find no one hiding behind those brocade panels. She had barely placed the cut-glass plate overflowing with preserved fruits and vegetables on the tablecloth when Aunt Viv shook her wooden-handled dinner bell.

The raucous-sounding bell had begun its life not at some fine eating establishment, but in a schoolyard. For over fifty years, Aunt Viv had taught fourth grade at the local elementary. As she told the story, when it was time for the students to return to the classroom each day after recess, she would vigorously swing the bell. She said it was next to impossible for a child to ignore a school bell's metal cup and clapper summons.

And at this moment, thought Mel as her relatives poured into the dining room, *no one in the house is ignoring its ringing call to dinner.*

§

fter the initial rush to fill plates, many members of the Crosby, Dare, and Kent families found space to eat at the over-sized table placed for Christmas in the center of the parlor. Others found a spot to sit and balance dinner on their laps on one of the couches, benches, stools or chairs scattered around the parlor, living room, dining room, and sun porch. The hubbub of the kitchen quieted, except for the occasional trip by Olivia to the stove to refill the gravy boat. The sound of voices, laughter, and Christmas music was punctuated by the chink of silverware against china and the rattle of ice in beverage glasses as toasts were made to the cooks, to the holiday, and to departed family members.

Mel sat on the cedar chest next to the foyer, nibbling on a wheat roll, and surveyed the rooms. From her vantage point everyone seemed happily engaged in conversation and eating. Everyone except for her Great-Uncle Clay.

Uncle Clay was Granny's brother-in-law. He had been married to Granny's eldest sister June for over sixty years. June had died early last spring, and he'd just put their home up for sale three weeks ago. Mel supposed he had chosen to sit in the Adirondack chair in the corner of the sun porch because it was beside a colorfully tinted picture of June and him. Or maybe, he'd selected that location to enjoy dinner because it had an unobstructed view of the Christmas tree.

Uncle Clay picked that instant to look over at Mel and caught her staring at him. Her great uncle squinted, leaned forward slightly, then beckoned. She nodded, stood, and proceeded to the sun porch, pausing on the way to deposit her used plate and silverware in the kitchen sink.

"Sit and enjoy the tree," said Uncle Clay as he patted a leather footstool positioned next to his Adirondack chair. "It is a beauty this year."

"I can see that." Mel studied the towering spruce festooned with antique glass balls, strings of white lights, strands of beads, old-fashioned tin garland, and shiny bells.

Aunt Viv only used antique ornaments. When the ones from Viv's childhood broke, she scoured rummage sales for appropriate replacements. Beneath the tree, her great aunt had arranged a village of glittery cardboard and wooden houses on top of a fluffy cotton blanket. The miniature Alpine village populated by metal people and animals, was surrounded by cone-shaped brush-bristle and wood evergreen trees.

Mel had heard stories that years ago, there had been a train, too. Whatever happened to train and tracks, no one seemed to know. Mel suspected that if she searched the corners of the attic, closets, and basement of the house on Park and Millstone, she would be able to locate the missing Lionel engine, cars, and circular track. It was common knowledge that Aunt Viv never discarded anything that had belonged to her parents, grandparents, great-grandparents, or other ancestors back to the Mayflower. And maybe some of the relics secreted away in the house predated the voyage to America. Maybe they were talismans from the European homelands of the oldest roots of the family.

But the real charm of Aunt Viv's tree wasn't the baubles or mini village—it was the evergreen itself. Every winter, accompanied by Olivia and Lill, she would snag a nephew or kindhearted neighbor to handle the trunk-sawing, and trudge through one of the local woodlands searching for the perfect Christmas tree. Locating a free or nearly free tree was a habit developed in Viv's childhood when the Crosbys had little spare cash. Now, though her great aunt could afford to go to a local lot and buy a tree, she continued the annual pilgrimage to the forest.

Once a tree was harvested, brought back to the house on Park and Millstone, and set up on the sun porch, the real work began. Aunt Viv had the uncanny ability to always select a tree that had numerous branchless spots on its trunk, which left large gaps between the needled fronds. Dissatisfied with the sparseness of the greenery, she'd go out into her yard and lop off wheelbarrows full of evergreen boughs to *fill in*. The species of pine, spruce, fir, hemlock, cedar, yew, boxwood, or holly made no difference to Mel's great-aunt. Evergreens were evergreens.

First, Aunt Viv would drill holes into the Christmas tree's trunk wherever she felt there ought to be thicker foliage. Next, she'd select a spray from the piles of mismatched branchlings, whittle its stem to the correct diameter, dip it in wood glue, and stick it in the hole. The drill, whittle, glue, and attach process would continue until she was pleased with the tree's fullness. Finally, she would trim any limbs that stuck out too far. The finished product was a perfectly shaped tree of many different needles and leaves. First time viewers of Vivian's Christmas tree were often puzzled as to what species of plant it was. And of course, never one to waste anything, the greens that remained after the tree was completed were used to decorate the house from cellar to attic.

"I especially like the holly and boxwood section near the rear," commented Mel.

"Yes, that is a particularly nice part this year. Reminds me of this family, different sorts glued together to make a fine looking tree." Uncle Clay chuckled. "If only all the branches were still here," he added softly, then turned his face to gaze out the window.

Melinda waited for her uncle to continue. She noted his complexion seemed more sallow, his cheekbones more pronounced, and his wrists and neck seemed thinner.

Uncle Clay cleared his throat, sighed, then looked at Mel.

She had noticed her great-uncle had barely touched his dinner. "Can I get you anything?"

He shook his head, glanced again out the window which now had snow piled on the outside of the windowsill and pane dividers.

"What are you looking at?"

"The woods across Millstone, down towards Oaks Corner Road." He adjusted his hearing aide, pushed his wire-rimmed glasses back into place.

"Every time I see that woods, it makes me think of Junie. Your Great-Aunt June, that is." After hesitating a second or two to wipe a minute dust particle from his spectacles, he proceeded, "She has been dead for seven months, now. I miss her terribly."

Mel looked out the window at the snow-covered landscape. Illuminated by streetlights, porch lights, and strings of holiday lights, it looked like a Currier and Ives painting. As if to complete the nostalgic scene, a pale owl flew past the window and into Aunt Viv's dilapidated barn. She glanced back at the lined face of her great-uncle.

"Why does that woods remind you of Aunt June?"

Behind the thick glass lenses, Uncle Clay's brown eyes seemed to brighten as he began his story. "Junie was fifteen, and I was seventeen. She had beautiful chestnut hair, just a little darker than yours." He smiled at Mel, then continued. "I saw her every week at church. Her parents were farmers, and only came to town on Sundays and once or twice a month to buy supplies at Phelps General Store."

He paused, looked out the window again, then resumed speaking: "I was afraid to talk to most of the girls. In those days, I stuttered badly. But Junie never seemed to mind. She was always laughing and friendly. Smart, too! Just a few years later, she taught over at the Elementary with your Aunt Viv."

Reminded of her aunt, Melinda tilted her head and listened to hear if the women were calling her to help clean up, yet. But there was still nothing but dinner chatter.

Her great-uncle noted her momentary distraction. "You don't have to listen to an old man if you have got better things to do."

"No. Go on. I was just making sure Aunt Viv didn't need me in the kitchen," she said, and touched her uncle's forearm.

He patted her hand. "As I was saying, I was shy. It took a lot of courage, but that December I asked her to the church hayride and bonfire." He paused, stared at the snowflakes coming down on the other side of the frosted panes. "And she said, 'Yes.'" He clapped his hands once for emphasis.

"I went to pick Junie up for the hayride at her parent's dairy farm in a sleigh. I had polished the harness leather and silver bells until they looked almost new, and brushed Jack, our black gelding, until he shone like obsidian. When I pulled up to her parents' house, Junie was out the door and waiting on the porch before I could climb down from the sleigh. Her parents and younger sisters, including your Granny, waved to us as we pulled away."

He raised his hands up, and then, let them fall into his lap. "We were headed to church, bundled in scarves, coats, hats, thick socks, mittens, blankets, and whatnot. I was showing off—whistling and snapping the reins so Jack would trot faster. Unfortunately, when we turned a corner, the sleigh tipped and we tumbled out. We weren't hurt, just snow-covered. And Jack stood there snorting at us. But then, the most amazing thing happened—instead of being angry, Junie giggled and threw a snowball at me."

He pointed toward a distant grove of trees across Millstone Street. "And that is when I kissed Junie, in a snowbank with snowflakes clinging to our eyelashes. She was so beautiful that evening."

He rubbed his bristly mustache, straightened his glasses, and added," The last time I kissed Junie before she died, her hair instead of the moon was silver and tears instead of snow crystals glistened on her pale skin. And yet, her blue eyes were the same blue eyes that had looked at me lovingly seventy years before. You see," Uncle Clay looked into Mel's eyes, down at his hands, then back into her eyes. "She was more beautiful for our last kiss than for our first."

"Oh, Uncle Clay." Melinda gave her great-uncle a hug. "I hope I find someone to love me as much as you loved Aunt June."

Her uncle returned her hug, tapped her nose with his forefinger. "Love, Melinda. As much as I still love Junie."

"Melinda," Aunt Vivian called from the kitchen. "Has anyone seen Melinda?"

"Coming," Mel shouted. "That was a wonderful story." She kissed her great-uncle on his cheek. "Do you want me to take that for you?" she offered, and reached for Uncle Clay's untouched dinner.

"Yes, dear. I am not very hungry tonight."

As Mel stood, Uncle Clay laid his hand on her forearm, added, "You are a good girl. I can see a bit of all sides of the family in you. Just promise me, Melinda, to leave the ghosts here when you go back to the city. Take the memories, but leave the dead behind."

"Um, okay." She shrugged her shoulders. "I am not sure what you mean, maybe you can explain it to me after the dishes are done."

"Maybe," answered her great-uncle before he turned to stare out the window at the grove of bare trees at the corner of Millstone and Oaks Corner.

fter the last pot was scrubbed, the last piece of silverware washed, and the last dish dried, Mel wandered back to the sun porch to converse with her great-uncle. He was nowhere to be seen. She searched through the downstairs rooms, then jogged upstairs. As she hurried down the second floor hallway, the bathroom door closed on its own and the bells tied to her bedroom window's curtain rod jingled for no particular reason. She tried to ignore the prickly feeling on the back of her neck, and did a quick look-see of the area. No Uncle Clay.

Mel returned to the first floor, and finally asked Aunt Viv, "Has anyone seen Uncle Clay?"

Aunt Vivian, Olivia, and Lill checked with the dinner guests. No one remembered seeing Clay after Melinda had visited with him on the sun porch.

"What ever were you talking to him about?" said her great aunt. Suddenly, the house seemed quiet and all eyes were fixed on Mel.

"The snow, sleigh rides, and Aunt June."

Several of her relatives coughed. Others glared at her.

"She could not have known," said Vivian in an apologetic voice. Then, turning to Mel, she explained, "Clay has gone a bit soft in the head. He is not always certain what year it is, and has taken to wandering off. Talking about June makes it worse."

"He seemed fine to me," offered Mel in a soft voice.

"Well, he's not. And now, we have got to go find him," growled Dave, her nineteen year-old Kent cousin, as he headed for the foyer.

Eight adults and teens volunteered to search for Uncle Clay. It was decided if he was not found in the next thirty minutes, they would call the authorities.

"Take a flashlight, stay in pairs. He can't have gone far in this weather. And make sure to check every route back to his house on Main Street," Aunt Viv said as she pulled several flashlights from a drawer and handed them out.

Mel pulled on her boots, tapped Cousin Dave on the shoulder. "If it's all right, I will partner with you."

"Suit yourself."

"I think we should head down towards Millstone and Oaks Corner. Uncle Clay was recalling a..."

"A sleigh ride and first kiss." Dave stood up, pushed open the front door for Mel. "I know the story."

As she stepped out off the porch and into the snow, Mel heard the muffled sound of bells on the other side of the front door. "It's a wonder we did not notice him leaving. Those bells make a racket."

Dave ignored her, swept his flashlight across the ground. "You could be right." He gestured towards what appeared to be a faint set of footprints in the snow leading towards Millstone Street. "The others are checking Park, and both Church Street and Millstone leading to Main, so let's head towards Oaks Corner."

Though the snow had stopped falling, Mel found it difficult to slog along the side of the roadway. It was a powdery snow, and had already begun to drift.

"Slow down, please," she begged her cousin.

"Here," he said and offered her his gloved hand.

"Thanks," she replied. "I am sorry I stirred up so much..." Mel paused. She heard the ting-a-linging of bells in the distance. Sleigh bells.

"Oh, no! Hurry!" She tugged on her cousin's hand. "Hurry, or he won't be there."

"I don't understand what..."

"You don't have to, but believe me when I say he will not be there if we don't hurry."

Without argument or further questions, the cousins ran and slipped towards the cluster of barren deciduous trees at the intersection of Millstone and Oaks Corner. Mel spotted a pair of barn owls perched on an oak bough, and thought she saw someone moving between the tree trunks. The music of sleigh bells was suddenly louder.

"Do you hear the bells? The jingling of silver bells on a leather harness?"

"Yeah. Actually, I do," answered Dave. "And it almost sounds as if there's a horse trotting..."

"On a snow-covered road," finished Mel. "The horse is snorting and the bells are ringing and..." She felt her eyes stinging from the wind and tearing up. "And their music is growing fainter. I think we're too late."

"No we're not. I can see Uncle Clay leaning against a tree." Her cousin released Mel's hand and raced ahead of her.

Dave was kneeling by Uncle Clay when she finally caught up to him. "He's dead," Dave said, and stood up.

"I knew he was gone. I knew it before we got here." She was careful to use the word *gone*. *Dead* did not seem the correct term. *Gone* was fitting. *Gone on a sleigh ride with Junie.*

Her cousin shook his head. "What a way to end a merry family reunion." He tugged his knit hat further down over his ears. "You wait with Uncle Clay, and I will go get help." Dave shoved his hands in his pockets, glanced at her one more time, then began the hike back to Aunt Vivian's house.

There was a reunion of the most magical kind tonight, thought Mel as she looked at Uncle Clay's peaceful face. *Though only I realize it.*

Then, Melinda, the girl who promised her great-uncle earlier tonight she would leave the ghosts with Aunt Viv at the house on Park and Millstone, whispered to the owls, the trees, the wind, the moon, the stars, and the spirits who roamed, "Merry Christmas to all, and to all, a good night."

Owls' Lullaby

Sail home, beautiful hunters,
with your fringed feathers muffling sound —
the moon has set
and the birds of dawn have begun
their sweet aubade.

Settle in, mysterious denizens of night,
in an abandoned house or hollow tree
for your diurnal sleep —
the sky has already swallowed the stars
and morning draws near.

Close your forward-seeing eyes,
magical fortune tellers,
and listen for daybreak's footsteps
with your flatten facial disks
and asymmetrical ears.

Dream away the bright hours,
legendary birds.
Then, awaken with the evening breezes
and flood the air
with your haunting prognostications.

About the Author

Born in the Year of the Dragon, *Vonnie Winslow Crist*, BS Art-Education and MS Professional Writing, has had a life-long interest in reading, writing, art, myth, fairy tales, folklore, legends, and science fiction. Her speculative writing has been nominated for Pushcart Awards and won several Writers of the Future Contest Honorable Mentions, a Maryland State Arts Council Grant, National League of American Pen Women Writing Contests, and other awards. A cloverhand who has found so many 4-leafed clovers she keeps them in jars, Vonnie believes the world around us is filled with miracles, mystery, and magic. Check her website: www.vonniewinslowcrist.com for more information about Vonnie and her writing and art.

Acknowledgments

Thanks to Kelly A. Harmon, Katie Hartlove, Michelle D. Sonnier for their friendship and invaluable critiquing, Wendy Stevens for her encouragement, and Pole to Pole Publishing for taking a another chance. Thank you to Patti Kinlock, the Baltimore Science Fiction Society, Balticon, and Broad Universe for supporting my forays into science fiction and fantasy. Again, thanks to my former instructors and classmates in Towson University's Professional Writing Masters Program for helping me grow as a writer—most especially, Dr. John L. Flynn. And as ever, thank you to my friends and family for supporting my creative endeavors and patiently listening to me spin tales about the mysterious and magical. Lastly, a special thanks to Ernie for always being there.

Praise for *The Greener Forest*
by
Vonnie Winslow Crist

The Greener Forest is that magical place where Faerie and the everyday world collide. There is dark and light, evil and good, and uncertain dusky gray lurking between its pages. Discover all is not what it seems at first glance, and wondrous things still happen in The Greener Forest.

"An intriguing look at the diverse relationships between humans and fairies. A wonderful, imaginative, multifaceted collection." – EJ Stevens, author of the Hunter's Guild urban fantasy series, Spirit Guide young adult series, and Ivy Granger urban fantasy series.

"Vonnie Winslow Crist's prose is simple, yet evocative, breathing life into all the wondrous creatures of Fairie. Read this collection. You won't be disappointed." – Robert E Waters, author of the Assassin's Lament Series

"Magickal, enchanting and so enticing. I was pulled in and couldn't stop reading!" -- TJ Perkins, author of the Shadow Legacy fantasy adventure series, The Kim & Kelly Mystery Series, and Four Little Witches.

Buy it now:

http://poletopolepublishing.com/books/the-greener-forest/

The Enchanted Dagger
The Chronicles of Lifthrasir, Volume 1
by
Vonnie Winslow Crist

Fourteen-year-old Beck Conleth is living a quiet life in the seaside town of Queen's Weather when his grandmother sends him on a journey to Ulfwood to retrieve his father's bones and a family dagger. After reaching Ulfwood, Beck discovers the dagger is magical, and that it answers only to him. Soon the enchanted dagger and its owner attract the attention of dark mages, goblins, and worse. Helped on his journey home by Wisewomen, warriors, shape-changers, and the other good folk of Lifthrasir, Beck faces death, danger, and the theft of his dagger. Accompanied by his best friend, Beck stows away on a ship, takes back his dagger, befriends a dragon, and escapes with a troop of thieves. After reaching a dock in West Arnora, the company heads for the fortress of Ravens Haunt. As Beck and his companions face a hideous Skullsoul and an army of ogrehunches, he realizes there is a developing confrontation between good and evil, and he and his enchanted dagger have a role to play.

"Adventure, magical creatures, enchantment, and evil lurking around every corner...a very enjoyable read." – Aimee Brown, reviewer

"A thrilling story...recommended to all readers of fantasy and adventure. Five stars and a thumbs-up to an excellent book." – Ellen Fritz, reviewer

Buy it Now:
http://poletopolepublishing.com/books/the-enchanted-dagger/

www.ingramcontent.com/pod-product-compliance
Lightning Source LLC
Chambersburg PA
CBHW020956180626
46814CB00003B/1120